It Takes Two

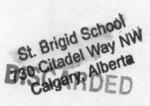

Other books by Bernice Thurman Hunter

Two Much Alike
Booky: A Trilogy
     That Scatterbrain Booky
     With Love from Booky
     As Ever, Booky
A Place for Margaret
Margaret in the Middle
Margaret on her Way
Lamplighter
The Railroader
The Firefighter
Hawk and Stretch
Amy's Promise
Janey's Choice
The Runaway

Bernice Thurman Hunter

It Takes Two

Cover art by
Ginette Beaulieu

Scholastic Canada Ltd.

Toronto New York London Auckland Sydney
Mexico City New Delhi Hong Kong Buenos Aires

Scholastic Canada Ltd.
175 Hillmount Rd., Markham, Ontario Canada L6C 1Z7

Scholastic Inc.
555 Broadway, New York NY 10012, USA

Scholastic Australia Pty Limited
PO Box 579, Gosford, NSW 2250, Australia

Scholastic New Zealand Ltd.
Private Bag 94407, Greenmount, Auckland, New Zealand

Scholastic Publications Ltd.
Villiers House, Clarendon Avenue, Leamington Spa,
Warwickshire CV32 5PR, UK

National Library of Canada Cataloguing in Publication

Hunter, Bernice Thurman
  It takes two / Bernice Thurman.
ISBN 0-7791-1389-6
  I. Title.
PS8565.U577I8 2002   jC813'.54   C2002-901882-X
PZ7

6 5 4 3 2 1   Printed in Canada   02 03 04 05 06

For Krystal, my favourite fan.

Contents

1. Good News? 1
2. Birthday Plans 4
3. Thirteen Candles 10
4. Aunt Sylvia Helps 14
5. A Long Hot Summer 19
6. The Middle of the Night 24
7. The Kicker 28
8. Homecoming .31
9. A Ruined Vacation 34
10. Marilyn's Plans .41
11. Eighth Grade 47
12. Wedding Plans .53
13. Wedding Bells .57
14. The House of Beauty 61
15. The Christmas Play 66
16. Christmas Eve, 1955 74
17. Christmas Day .78
18. Duplicity 82
19. A Knock at the Door 91
20. Easter in Toronto 97
21. The Old Mill 102
22. Holiday 109
23. Home Again 117
24. Aunt Sylvia's 121

25. Fourteen 124
26. The Switcheroo 130
27. A Sunday Drive 133
28. Wonderful News 141
29. Happy Birthday, Babies! 146
30. Summer Jobs 149
31. Queen for a Day 152
32. Identical Thoughts 155
33. A Miracle 162

Chapter 1

Good News?

"Darn!" Carrie flopped back on the bottom bunk and heaved a big sigh. "Jimmy's finally grown up enough to act like a normal human being . . . and now this!"

This was the "good news" our parents had just told us at the supper table.

"Your mother's expecting," Dad had announced proudly.

"Expecting what?" Jimmy had asked. He was normal, but dumb.

"A baby, of course," laughed Mom, rolling her eyes at her youngest. "You're going to have a new brother or sister."

We had noticed that Mom was getting a bit fat but we thought it was just the middle-age spread.

"Imagine . . . at their age." I snorted. "Mom's nearly forty-three years old and Dad's forty-six! I thought it was practically impossible at that age."

"It's worse than impossible," muttered Carrie. "Do you realize what it means?"

"Don't say it!" I plugged my ears with my fingers. "I don't even want to think about it!"

I turned and peered at myself in the dresser mirror. Carrie bounced up and stood beside me. Leaning closer to the glass, we began picking at twin pimples on our chins.

"What will all our friends say?" Carrie scowled in the mirror. "Especially Lorena!" Lorena Ellsworth was an only child and proud of it.

"I wonder how Robbie feels about it?" I said. "He didn't say anything when Dad told us. And he's nearly seventeen. What will his friends say?"

"Oh, boys don't care." Carrie handed me a Kleenex and we dabbed at the red spots on our chins. "After all, they don't have to babysit, do they? And dopey Jimmy said he didn't care as long as it's a boy."

"A baby sister might be nice," I said. "Nancy Case's baby sister, Martha, is a real doll."

"Yes, but Nancy's mother is still in her thirties. That's different." Carrie marched off to the bathroom. I followed her and we washed our faces with Noxzema and covered the red spots with Clearasil.

"Why would Mom and Dad want a baby at their age?" I puzzled.

Carrie glanced at me in the bathroom mirror and I got that spooky feeling that identical twins get . . . as if seeing yourself through someone else's eyes.

"Well," Carrie puckered her eyebrows. "When we were at Aunt Sylvia's house last Sunday I heard her say something to Uncle Phil that I didn't understand. But it's beginning to make sense now."

"What makes sense now?"

"Aunt Sylvia said it was probably an accident."

"An accident! How could a baby be an accident?"

We went back to our room and got into our PJs.

"What else could it be, Connie?"

"I think it's more like Sarah Rafter's little brother, Jordan. Sarah's mother calls him her 'change of life surprise'!"

We knew all about the change of life. Aunt Sylvia had a *Medical Home Advisor* — a big thick book almost the size of the Detroit telephone directory — on her coffee table, along with her books on nutrition and exercise. Carrie and I had both browsed through that book when we used to mind Ronnie.

Ronnie was Aunt Sylvia's boy who never grew up. He had been chronologically the same age as our Jimmy. But Mom had explained that he'd always be a baby in his mind, and we were never to question Aunt Sylvia about him. So we never did.

There was a chapter in the book all about the change of life. The book explained that it was something that happens to women between the ages of 40 and 50, and said that the proper name for it was "the menopause." I wondered why it was called *men*-opause if it only happened to women. Anyway, Mom was right in that age group. She would be forty-three on May 16th, 1955, the same day that Carrie and I would become teenagers!

Thirteen! It was the birthday we had been looking forward to all our lives. But now . . . who knew what was going to happen? Our whole family could be completely spoiled, ruined, decimated (Carrie's word) by a squalling, squealing, pooping, peeing baby!

Chapter 2

Birthday Plans

As our birthday drew closer, Mom grew round as a barrel. Dad called her Mrs. Five-by-Five. Mom usually rolled her eyes and laughed at Dad's jokes, but lately she seemed to have lost her sense of humour. "That's not funny!" she had snapped at him. Then, when Jimmy, who was a natural born mimic, asked her in a perfect imitation of Dad's voice, "What's for supper, Mrs. Five-by-Five?" she wheeled around and clipped him on the ear.

"*Oww!*" Jimmy squealed, grabbing his ear. "What did you do that for?"

Jimmy was Mom's baby and he'd never been hit in his life. Not by Mom anyway.

"You watch your saucy tongue," Mom snapped at him. "I demand a little respect around here."

So Carrie and I knew better than to expect a birthday party this year, which was a horrible disappointment because it would have been our first mixed party, both boys and girls, and we had been looking forward to it forever.

4

"Already he's ruining everything," grumbled Carrie on our way home from school.

"Maybe he's a she," I suggested.

"I've got a feeling it's a boy," Carrie said.

"I've got a feeling it's a girl," I said.

Then I thought, that's funny, us having opposite feelings. Being identical twins, we nearly always felt exactly the same. Aunt Sylvia said sometimes we were positively clairvoyant. Like the time, a couple of years ago, when Dad had the accident in "Boris Karloff." Boris Karloff was the name our brother, Robbie, had given our old 1946 Ford station wagon. Anyway, Dad was late for supper that night, which was not like him at all. Mom always said you could set your clock to the very minute that our dad walked in the door — 5:30 — so she had covered his plate with an upside-down pie pan and put it in the oven to keep warm.

"Where could your father be?" She had kept checking the kitchen clock. Then Carrie and I had both said at once, "He's probably had an accident." And he had. Another driver had rear-ended him and Dad got whiplash and the back end of Boris Karloff had been smashed to smithereens. The other driver had actually admitted that it was his fault so Dad had got a plaster-of-Paris collar for his neck and an almost new — 1951 — Ford station wagon. Free! Dad wouldn't drive any car but a Ford. He was a Ford man for life, he said, ever since Henry Ford had given him a job during the Great Depression when jobs were as scarce as a newborn baby's teeth. Robbie had instantly named the new car Flash Gordon because it had flashy silver streaks down the sides.

"Instead of a party," Mom said, sitting down to catch her breath, "how would you like to take two of your friends out to dinner and the show?"

"Two each?" we asked.

"I guess so."

"Okay," we agreed before she could change her mind. "Can we pick the restaurant?"

"Can I come?" butted in Jimmy.

"No!" we snapped.

"How about Foster's Fish and Chips?" Mom said. Mom always picked fish-and-chip shops because she was English.

"Yuck!" gagged Jimmy, sticking his finger down his throat.

"Yuck! Yuck!" For once we agreed with our little brother.

"How about that new restaurant, Chicken Joy?" Robbie suggested. He had just come in the back door and dropped his huge science book, with a thump, on the kitchen table.

"You can't come to our party!" we yelled at him.

"I'd rather jump off a cliff!" snorted Robbie.

"Can I come if I promise not to talk?" Jimmy tried again.

"Not even if you make yourself invisible," Carrie and I said.

"Stop your wrangling, all of you!" Mom pushed herself up by the table's edge. "And clear out of my kitchen. Your father will be home in less than an hour and I haven't even started supper yet."

All four of us high-tailed it into the front room and

argued about what to watch on television. Then Robbie settled the argument by getting the corn broom from the closet and making us all pull a straw. The short straw won, and it was Jimmy's.

"Yay!" he hollered, cranking the knob on the Motorola to channel four.

We could get three other channels on our giant seventeen-inch screen since Dad had installed a rotor. When you turned the rotor wheel on top of the cabinet, it made the aerial on the roof rotate with a screechy sound, like fingernails on a blackboard, and a new channel would come into focus.

* * *

That night Carrie and I had twin headaches. Dr. Mary Duncan, our family doctor, had diagnosed our headaches as migraines. But Mom had her own diagnosis.

"It's probably from watching too much television," she said. "It's enough to burn the eyes right out of your head."

"That's just an old wives' tale," Dad said. "It sounds like something my mother would have said to me when I was a boy."

"Well, there was no television when you were a boy, so she wouldn't have said it, now would she?"

Dad cracked open the *Detroit Free Press* and buried his nose in it. Mom gave Carrie and me each a glass of foaming Bromo-Seltzer and sent us to bed.

I leaned over the rail of the upper bunk and looked down at Carrie. The gold flecks in her green eyes sparkled in the glow of the streetlight coming in under the window blind.

"Who are you going to invite, Carrie?" I asked.

She ran her fingers through her long, wavy brown hair, spread out like a fan on the pillow. It was our best feature, our hair.

"I think I'll ask two boys from our class," she said.

We were in the same classroom this year, seventh grade. Up until now we had always been separated to avoid confusion. No one could tell us apart except our family, and even they were fooled sometimes. The only way to tell for sure was a family secret. It was our ears. I had a bent right ear and Carrie had a bent left ear. That's because we're mirror twins. But we both wore our hair long so nobody ever saw our ears, anyway.

"You can't ask two boys. Mom won't let you."

"Well, I'm going to, anyway. So you can ask two girls and that'll make it even."

"I'm not asking two girls. I'll ask one of each."

"Which boy do you want then?"

I didn't hesitate for a second. "Hunter Davidson," I said.

"No!" Carrie bobbed up in bed and glared at me. "I'm asking Hunter. You know I've got a crush on him."

"Well, so have I."

That was the problem. Our taste in boys was exactly alike. "Let's toss a coin," I said. That was how we often settled our differences.

Carrie hopped out of bed and clicked on the lady lamp on the dresser. I swung down from the top bunk. There was a nickel beside the lamp's ceramic pink skirt.

Carrie placed the nickel on top of her thumbnail. "Heads or tails?" she said.

"Heads," I said.

She flipped the coin off her thumb and it landed,

tails up, on the bedroom mat.

"Two out of three," I said.

"Oh, Connie, there must be another boy you like."

"Well . . . Jason Gallagher's sorta cute," I said. "And he's Hunter Davidson's best friend."

"Okay," Carrie crawled back into bed. "And we'll all be together anyway."

I clicked off the lamp and climbed up the ladder to my bunk. "What girl do you want to ask? Not Pamela Potter, I hope."

"Heck no. She wouldn't even want to come to our party. She's got a bunch of new friends now."

Pamela Potter had been Carrie's best friend last year. But ever since the accident, when Carrie had been badly hurt in Pam's dad's car (she had needed a transfusion and my identical blood had saved her life) their friendship had cooled off.

"I think I'll ask Nancy Case," I said. "Nancy's about my best friend this year." Last year Wendy Johnson had been my best friend but she had moved away to Port Huron.

"Okay," Carrie agreed. "And I'll invite Lorena Ellsworth. Do you like her okay?"

"Sure," I said.

Then Carrie said, "Ginny-winny-ninny-gite," with a loud yawn.

"Ginny-winny-ninny-gite," I answered.

That meant goodnight in Twinnish. Twinnish was our own special language that we had invented when we were young. It sounded childish now that we were in junior high, so we didn't use it much anymore.

Chapter 3

Thirteen Candles

"I won't be able to take you shopping for your present this year," Mom said, her hands clasped over her stomach. It was the Saturday morning of our party. "So here's your birthday money." She handed us each a ten-dollar bill.

We went downtown by bus in the afternoon. Downtown Detroit was seething with shoppers because all the spring clearance sales were on.

We were standing in the doorway of Stella's Styles for Mature Women, laughing our heads off at the mannequins in the window wearing funny, old-lady dresses, when a mature woman behind us snapped, "Well . . . are you going in?"

"We'd rather jump off a cliff!" we screeched.

"Cheeky brats!" she snapped, pushing past us.

Carrie and I made cheeky faces at her back. Then Carrie said, "Are you getting a dress or a suit?"

"I don't know. But I'm going to Hudson's. It's my favourite store."

"Okay, then I'll go to Crowley's."

So we went our separate ways, promising to meet at the bus stop in an hour.

On the bus we didn't look into each other's bags. When we got home, we dumped our new outfits out on Carrie's bed. They turned out to be exactly the same: fern-green corduroy suits that matched our eyes exactly.

"Oh, no!" we both groaned. We didn't have time to exchange them — we had to hurry because the two boys and two girls we had invited were due at our house in an hour — so we decided on different-coloured blouses.

Dad drove the lot of us to Chicken Joy in Flash Gordon. Then he went up to the counter and paid for our dinners. Chicken Joy had a sign in the window: one price includes everything.

A lady wearing a chicken apron led us to a table with a bench on both sides. A bouquet of chicken balloons floated above the table. It was tethered to a chicken-shaped bowl, full of rolls, in the middle of the table. Carrie and I slid onto the bench on either side of Hunter. Jason managed to squeeze in beside me. So Lorena and Nancy had to sit on the opposite bench with no boy in between.

Two waiters dressed in rooster costumes came flapping to our table with baskets of fried chicken and chips. At the end of the dinner, they came flapping back again carrying two cakes flaming with thirteen candles each. Then they sang "Happy Birthday" at the top of their lungs, and they finished by crowing, "Cock-a-doodle-doo!"

We both managed to blow out all our candles.

When the cakes were all gone down to the last crumb our guests gave us our presents: the boys gave us each a

Doris Day record (mine was "Secret Love") and the girls gave us Five Year Daily Journals.

Then it was off to the Cinderella Theater, just around the corner. Dad had already bought us our tickets.

There was a double bill playing that night: *Singing In the Rain* and *Roman Holiday*. Both were billed as romantic comedies.

We were a bit late so we couldn't all sit together. Lorena and Nancy had to sit in the front row. Then the usher found two seats in the back row for Jason and me, and two seats at the opposite end of the back row for Carrie and Hunter.

I knew Jason from school, but we'd never been alone before. Halfway through the first movie, when Gene Kelly was singing his head off in the rain, Jason grabbed hold of my hand. I didn't know what to do so I didn't do anything. Then, during a romantic moment in *Roman Holiday*, he squeezed my fingers. Suddenly he leaned over and stuck out his lips. I turned my face away but he still hung onto my hand and he didn't let go until the end of the show when the lights flared on.

Lorena and Nancy looked miffed when we met in the lobby. As if it was our fault that they had had to sit in the front row. Carrie and Hunter were laughing at something and Carrie was rolling her eyes like Mom.

Dad met us out front under the marquee.

"Did everybody have a good time?" he asked.

"Yes, thank you!" we chorused.

Then he took everybody home in Flash Gordon.

Mom was waiting for us in the kitchen. "I hope you weren't too disappointed about not having your teenage party," she said.

12

"Maybe next year," Dad said. They both sounded so apologetic that we felt sorry for them.

"No, we weren't disappointed," we assured them. "It was lots more fun than a party."

* * *

Hours later, when I was sure Carrie was asleep, and I was on the verge of sleep myself, she suddenly whispered in the darkness, "Did Jason try to kiss you?"

I sat up so fast I bumped my head on the ceiling. "Yes," I whispered, rubbing my head. "But I didn't let him."

"Why?"

"I don't know. I guess I don't like him that much. Did Hunter try to kiss you?"

"Sure."

"Did you let him?"

"Sure!"

"What was it like?" I felt a pang of jealousy.

"Okay, I guess. It was my first kiss so I don't have anything to compare it to."

"Darn!" I flopped back on my pillow. "I guess I should have let Jason kiss me, too, even if I don't like him that much. Then we would've both got our first kiss on the same night."

We laughed, then I said, "Hey," thinking about the cakes with the thirteen candles, "what did you wish for, Carrie?"

"Oh, just that I'd pass this year with honours."

"Me, too," I said, yawning. "Ginny-winny-ninny— "

"No more Twinnish," Carrie interrupted. "It's baby talk, and we're teenagers now. Goodnight."

"Goodnight," I said reluctantly. I hated to give up Twinnish altogether.

Chapter 4

Aunt Sylvia Helps

Mom was expecting the baby near the end of July. It seemed strange to come home from school and find her lying on the sofa. Usually she was buzzing around the house like a honeybee. But lately she had changed. Not just physically but mentally, too. Mom hardly ever watched television in the daytime. She said most soap-box stories were soppy and people who watched them were dim. And game shows were even worse. But now she was always on the sofa watching *The Guiding Light* or *Strike it Rich.*

One day we got home late. We had been dawdling along Jefferson Avenue with Hunter and Jason and didn't realize what time it was. Ever since our birthday they were sort of our boyfriends. We still both liked Hunter best but we agreed not to fight about it.

We said goodbye to them at the corner and sprinted up Newport Street. When we got near our house we recognized Aunt Sylvia's beige and brown two-tone Chevrolet parked at the curb, and we dashed up our front walk.

We both loved Aunt Sylvia, even though she wasn't really our aunt — she was Mom's best friend. Our real aunts, dad's sisters, lived in Toronto, Canada, and Mom had a half-sister in England who we had never seen. So Aunt Sylvia was our favourite.

Bursting into the hall, we let the door slam behind us. Aunt Sylvia came running down the stairs.

"Shh!" She pressed her finger to her lips. "Your mother is resting."

Usually she met us with a big smile. But today she looked solemn as a preacher.

"Is Mom sick?" we asked anxiously.

"No. Just tired. Let's go start the supper."

We frowned at each other and followed her into the kitchen.

No-one ever made supper at our house but our mom. She was very possessive about her kitchen.

Aunt Sylvia had brought a tuna-fish casserole with buttered crumbs on top. She put it into the oven and got the salad stuff out of the Frigidaire: lettuce and celery and pale pink tomatoes in a cellophane package, the kind Dad hated. He said they were about as tasty as an old tennis ball.

"You two toss the salad while I stir the pudding," she said. "It's butterscotch tapioca." Then she added with a sigh, "It was my Ronnie's favourite."

Ronnie had passed away on New Year's Day. Mom said Aunt Sylvia would never get over losing him. Dad said he wasn't 'lost' and he didn't 'pass away' — he died. Dad was a realist. He hated euphemisms.

We were mixing the salad in a green glass bowl when Jimmy came in the kitchen door.

"HI, AUNT SYLVIA!" he hollered, excited to see her.

"Shhh!" she hushed him. "Be quiet!"

"Why?" His voice dropped to a whisper.

"'Cause Mom's resting in bed," Carrie and I said.

"Why?" Jimmy asked Aunt Sylvia.

Just then Robbie came in. He was about to drop his pile of books on the table the way he always did, to prove how hard he had to work in high school, when Aunt Sylvia wheeled around and cried, "Don't you dare!"

He set the books down quietly and asked, "What's wrong?"

"Nothing's wrong," Aunt Sylvia assured him. "Your mother is having a rest, that's all. I'm off work for a few days while my shop is being renovated," — Aunt Sylvia was a hairdresser and Uncle Phil had persuaded her to go back to work after Ronnie died — "so I thought I'd come over and give her a hand." She looked over her shoulder and gave us a big reassuring smile, one hand still stirring the pudding. "None of you seem very glad to see me," she said.

"Yes, we are!" Carrie and I jumped up and hugged her around her slim waist. Aunt Sylvia had always been thinner than our Mom. Mom said it was because she'd had only two children compared to four, and that twins were especially hard on the figure, but right now the difference was astounding.

"That's more like it," she smiled. Then she scraped the hot pudding into a Pyrex bowl. "Robbie, would you slide down to the corner store and get another quart of milk? I've used it all up in the pudding."

Robbie put his hand in the cracked sugar bowl where Mom kept her kitchen money. "C'mon, Sport," he said to

16

Jimmy. "I'll ride you down on my bike."

Jimmy loved going places with his big brother. Grinning from ear to ear, he followed him out the door.

The minute they were gone we bombarded our aunt with questions: "Is the baby going to be born soon? Does Dad know? Is Mom coming down for supper?"

"I thought we'd fix her a nice tray." Aunt Sylvia answered the last question, adroitly ignoring the others. "Fetch me that fancy tray from the dining-room wall."

The fancy tray was one of the few things that Mom had got from England. Her grandmother had sent it from Nottingham for a wedding present. Mom prized it so much she wouldn't use it, so Dad had hung it on the wall like a picture.

The tray was oval with handles at each end. The oval was covered in glass and under it was a beautiful Nottingham lace doily. The tray was surprisingly heavy, so we carried it between us and set it carefully on the counter.

Aunt Sylvia made the tray look pretty as a picture with Mom's best china. The small heap of golden-brown tuna casserole, a spoonful of shiny green peas, and a spoonful of grated carrots topped with a sprig of parsley looked so good Carrie and I were salivating as we carried it between us up the stairs. Aunt Sylvia followed with the teapot.

"Oh, Sylvia, you shouldn't have gone to all that trouble!" Mom protested as she pushed herself up to a sitting position.

"It was no trouble at all," Aunt Sylvia assured her.

There was hardly any room on Mom's lap, so we propped the tray in front of her on a pillow and held it steady by the handles on either side.

Aunt Sylvia set the teapot on the walnut dresser, on a magazine so it wouldn't make a white ring. "I'll be back with dessert," she said. "You twins make sure that your mother eats. She's going to need her strength."

Just then we heard the front door open and Dad called up the stairs, "Hello the house!" He always said that when he was in a jolly mood.

"We're up here, Dad!" we hollered and he came bounding up the stairs. He kissed Mom's cheek and he didn't seem surprised to see her being fed in bed.

After Mom finished her supper Dad picked up the tray and said, "Good girl!"

We couldn't believe our ears.

"I don't know what I ever did to deserve such service," Mom said. "Tell Sylvia I can't eat another bite."

"Oh, but she's made delicious tapioca pudding, Mom," we said.

"And you'll want your tea," Dad said.

"I'll have it later." Mom leaned back on the pillow and laced her fingers across her big round stomach. Little beads of sweat glistened on her forehead and black wispy curls stuck to her cheekbones.

"Kiss me goodnight in case I'm asleep when you come back," she said to us. "And send your brothers up."

Chapter 5

A Long Hot Summer

Summer vacation promised to be an awful drag that year. All four of us kids had passed our June exams with flying colours, but Dad said we couldn't do anything special to celebrate because of Mom's "condition."

Aunt Sylvia had gone back to work but she came up every night for an hour or two. One night her daughter, Marilyn, came with her.

Marilyn was twenty years old and was considered an Irish beauty. (Her father, Uncle Phil, was half Irish on his mother's side.) Marilyn had thick strawberry-blonde hair, huge green eyes (not flecked with brown like ours) and dimples in both cheeks. And she had a shape that Carrie and I hoped to have some day. But we didn't really like her. For one thing she thought she was *sooo* sophisticated. And for another thing, our Robbie had a crush on her.

Marilyn was sitting in Dad's La-Z-Boy buffing her long red nails. It was a hot July night. Robbie had plugged in the fan and pointed it at Marilyn. He had brought the

19

fan downstairs because Mom said it gave her a chill.

Lifting her strawberry-blonde hair with her fingers to let the breeze blow on her long white neck, Marilyn cooed at Robbie, "Ooh, that's lovely." Then she looked at Carrie and me, sitting cross-legged in front of the television waiting for *Lassie* to come on. "Why don't you two kids run down to the store and get us a bottle of ginger ale?" she said.

"We're not kids," we snapped. "And we have no money."

"Oh, that's no problem now that I'm a working girl." She reached for her purse on the floor.

Then Robbie said, "Heck no, it's my treat," and he fished some change out of his pants pocket. "Here's fifty cents. Get two bottles," he said.

"Last of the big time spenders," Carrie and I snickered.

"Turn the television to another channel," Marilyn ordered Robbie. "I don't like kiddie shows." He obeyed without batting an eye.

So off we went down Newport Street to get the ginger ale.

Detroit was in the middle of a heat wave and the whole neighbourhood was sitting out on their verandas fanning themselves. As we passed the Mortimers' house, Mrs. Mortimer came flying down the veranda steps so fast she lost a slipper. Then she parked herself right in front of us with her arms folded and her feet apart so we couldn't get by. "Hello there, twins!" she cried. That's what lots of people called us instead of our names because they couldn't tell us apart. Mostly we didn't mind.

20

Mrs. Mortimer leaned so close her onion breath enveloped us like a cloud. "How's your poor dear mother?" she asked anxiously.

Our poor dear mother? What did she mean by that?

"She's fine," we said, trying to sidestep her.

"Well, I see her sister driving up the street every day of the week so there must be something wrong," she insisted.

"What sister?" we asked innocently.

Then, before another question could come out of her smelly mouth Carrie grabbed my arm and pulled me off the curb. A car speeding by honked its horn, and we leaped onto the sidewalk just past Mrs. Mortimer. From there we bolted down the street.

"You be sure to tell your mother that if she needs any help just to let me know!" Mrs. Mortimer called after us.

"Okay!" we called back. "Old Nosy Parker," we laughed derisively.

As we turned on to Jefferson Avenue we nearly bumped into Hunter Davidson and Jason Gallagher.

"Hi!" Hunter said. "Where are you going?"

"To the store," we said, "for ginger ale."

They fell into step on either side of us. "Do you two always talk like that?" Jason asked with a grin.

"Like what?" we said.

Hunter gave a snorty hoot. "Like that," he said. "Both at once."

"Not always," we said.

"Then let's see you quit doing it," Jason said.

"Okay," we said.

They walked with us to the corner store, kidding all the way. "Want an ice cream cone, Carrie?" Hunter tossed a quarter up in the air and caught it.

"I'm not Carrie," I said. "I'm Connie."

As soon as he knew which twin I was he changed over to Carrie's side and repeated the question.

Then Jason said, "I'll buy you an ice cream cone, Connie," as if he felt sorry for me.

"No thanks!" I snapped at him. Which wasn't fair because he was just trying to be nice. But why did Hunter like Carrie better than me, I wondered?

I waited impatiently while Carrie finished the double-decker cone Hunter had bought her. Then we went into the corner store for the ginger ale. When we came out the boys had gone off down the street with two other boys, so we walked home alone and I was all huffy.

"What's the matter with you?" Carrie snapped.

"That darn Hunter Davidson," I grumbled. "Who does he think he is? And why did you have to flirt with him?"

"I didn't flirt with him."

"You did."

"Didn't."

"Did too."

"Oh, shut up. I can't help it if he likes me better than you."

I had no answer to that because it was true. Maybe Carrie was nicer than me, I thought. It had to be something like that because it wasn't our looks. He couldn't even tell us apart.

When we got home we could see that Robbie was in a bad mood, too. He snatched the bottle of ginger ale out of my hand and began filling the coloured aluminum tumblers lined up on the counter.

"Where's Marilyn?" Carrie and I asked.

"You took so long she got bored and went home," he snapped.

"Here." He handed me a sweating red tumbler. "Take this up to Mom."

She was sitting up in bed and Aunt Sylvia was fixing her hair. Mom looked okay. Just too fat for words.

"Thank you, dears," she said. She took the cold red tumbler and sipped from it gratefully. Then she rolled it across her forehead.

When Aunt Sylvia had finished with Mom's hair, and Mom had finished her ginger ale, Aunt Sylvia pulled the two pillows out from behind Mom's back, punched them up, threw one over on to Dad's side and settled Mom back on her pillow.

"What day is it?" Mom asked.

"Friday," Carrie and I answered.

"No. I mean what day of the month," Mom said.

"It's July 15th," Aunt Sylvia said. "Anything else you need to know?"

"That'll do for now." Mom sighed and rubbed her stomach in circles. "I'll be glad when this is over," she said.

On the way downstairs I said, "So will I!" And Carrie said, *Moi aussi!* just to be different.

This baby business had just about ruined our summer so far. Not that we didn't enjoy having Aunt Sylvia come over nearly every day. But we wanted our Mom back to normal again.

Chapter 6

The Middle of the Night

I was dreaming that Carrie had strawberry-blonde hair and we weren't identical anymore when something woke me with a start. Rubbing my eyes I looked at our clock on the dresser with the green fluorescent face: twelve o'clock. Midnight. Then I heard a muffled cry from across the hall.

I leaned over the rail. "Carrie, are you awake?"

"Yes," she said.

"Did you hear that?"

"Yes." She got up and crept to the door. I swung down from the top bunk and followed her. We opened it a crack.

Just then Dad came out of our parents' bedroom, all dressed, went to the boys' room and opened the door. "Robbie!" He spoke in a loud whisper. "Get up and give me a hand."

"I'm asleep," mumbled Robbie drowsily.

"Wake up right now." Dad pushed open the door. "Your mother needs you."

Carrie and I ran into the hall. "Dad! Dad! What is it? Is Mom all right?"

"The baby's coming," he said.

"Shall we phone Aunt Sylvia?"

"No, no, we can manage," he said. "Robbie, you bring the suitcase from the closet. And you twins help your mother while I go get the car." The houses on Newport Street were built so close together that there was no room for driveways, so cars were parked in the back lane.

Mom was sitting on the edge of the bed all dressed, holding her stomach. We each grabbed an arm and helped her up. Then we guided her down the stairs, out the door, and down the veranda steps.

Dad had the car at the curb with its door open. He looked as if he was about to pick Mom up bodily and set her on the seat when she suddenly flailed her arms and shooed us all off like flies.

"Get away from me, all of you!" she cried. We backed off and she eased herself into the front seat, then heaved a big sigh. Dad closed the door and ran around to the driver's side and jumped in. Robbie threw the suitcase into the back seat.

The three of us stood on the sidewalk under the streetlight watching as Flash Gordon bore our parents away down Newport Street. Then the car disappeared around the corner onto Jefferson.

We turned and went silently back to the house. Carrie and I went in. Robbie stayed out on the veranda.

"Let's have some ginger ale," Carrie whispered.

"Okay," I whispered back.

She filled three tumblers and we went back out onto the veranda.

"Want a ginger ale?" we whispered to Robbie.

"Sure," he said. "But why are you whispering?"

We laughed nervously and sat down on either side of him on the glider. It creaked as Robbie pushed it with his feet.

We sat for a long time without talking. I knew exactly what Carrie was thinking because I could practically read her mind, but what was my big brother thinking? I wondered.

"What do you think, Robbie?" Carrie asked the question for me.

"About what?"

"About the baby."

"Aw, I've been through all this before," he said with a wave of his hand. "I remember when you guys were born."

"You don't," I said.

"You were only four years old," Carrie said.

"Yeah, well, I remember Dad coming home from the hospital and telling me I had two baby sisters and wasn't I lucky," he snorted.

"Did you like us?" we asked.

"Are you kidding?" he snorted again. "I don't even like you now. And when Jimmy came three years later, every night of the week I was planning to run away from home."

"Who ran away from home?" Jimmy was standing at the door in his PJs, blinking in the porch light. He had slept right through the commotion, which didn't surprise us a bit because he'd slept right through an earthquake once.

"Mom and Dad," Robbie teased. "They just packed up and left."

"In Flash Gordon?" Jimmy was serious.

"Sure." Robbie loved pulling his little brother's leg.

All of a sudden Jimmy burst into tears. "I don't want them to go," he blubbered. "Who'll make breakfast?"

The three of us burst out laughing and Jimmy cried even harder.

"Stop laughing!" he choked. "I didn't say anything funny."

Then Robbie said, "It's okay, Sport. Dad took Mom to the hospital to have the baby."

"Oh, is that all." Jimmy stopped crying on a dime. "Well, I hope it's a boy."

"Me too," agreed Robbie.

"Well, we hope it's a girl," Carrie said, switching to my side. We always did that when the chips were down.

Robbie got up and the glider swayed and creaked. "C'mon," he said, "let's all go back to bed."

Normally we would have put up an argument because we didn't like being bossed around by our big brother. But there was nothing normal about this night, so we followed him in and up the stairs. But it was hard to settle down and get back to sleep.

"Do you really care if it's a boy or girl?" I whispered to Carrie.

Carrie pondered my question. "Well . . . if it's a boy it will have to sleep in the boys' room . . . "

"Hmmm. I never thought of that." I sat up and bumped my head on the ceiling. "And if it's a girl we'll get stuck with it and our room's too crowded already. So it better be a boy."

"Exactly," agreed Carrie.

Chapter 7

The Kicker

Dad woke us at eight o'clock in the morning banging on our doors. "Everybody up!" he hollered. "I've got big news!"

All four of us staggered, bleary-eyed, into the hallway. And there was Dad grinning like a Cheshire cat, from ear to ear.

"What news?" cried Carrie and I.

"Is it breakfast time yet?" yawned Jimmy. "I'm starved."

"Is Mom okay, Dad?" asked Robbie anxiously.

"She'll be fine," Dad said. "All she needs now is rest."

"The news, Dad, the news!" we begged.

"Well . . ." he paused dramatically. "We've done it again!"

"Done what? Done what?" we screamed and jumped around, pulling at his shirtsleeves.

"We've got ourselves another set of twins," he announced triumphantly.

Twins! Carrie and I stared at each other.

"Boys or girls?" Robbie asked.

"Guess!" teased Dad.

"No, Dad, tell us!" Carrie and I begged.

"Well . . . hold on to your hats, because here comes the kicker: We've got one of each!"

"Really?"

"A boy and a girl?"

"That's right," Dad said, rubbing his hands together excitedly. "The boy weighed in at six pounds and the little girl at five."

"No wonder Mom was so fat," Jimmy whistled. "Twelve pounds of baby."

"Eleven, dummy," corrected Robbie. "Are they okay, Dad?"

"They're fine," Dad said. "Your mother had a Caesarean operation so she didn't feel a thing. But Dr. Duncan said she's keeping all three of them in the hospital for at least ten days, so you'll all have to pitch in around here. And now's a good time to start, so follow me."

We trundled after him down the stairs and into the kitchen. We'd never seen Dad like this before. He was positively elated!

"Let's make a bang-up big breakfast to celebrate," Dad said. He made cheese omelettes in the frying pan and we didn't even know he knew how.

Carrie and I set the table and Robbie made coffee in the percolator. Jimmy was in charge of the toaster.

We were finished eating and Dad was using a toothpick from the chicken-shaped eggcup in the middle of the table. Robbie poured us all a mug of coffee.

"Oh, boy!" cried Jimmy, stirring a big splash of cream.

"Mom never lets me have coffee. She says it'll stunt my growth." Then he looked at Dad over his steaming mug. "Are the twins identical, Dad?" he asked. He was serious!

Dad laughed so hard coffee shot out of his nose. Robbie gave a loud guffaw. "A boy and girl can't be identical, nitwit!" he hooted.

"It's biologically impossible," Carrie explained loftily.

"Thank goodness," I said.

Chapter 8

Homecoming

They didn't come home for thirteen days because both babies had the jaundice. When we first saw them they were still a bit yellow. Jimmy took one look into the cradle with a baby at each end and cried, "Yuck!"

Robbie looked at them curiously and didn't say a word.

Carrie and I said they were cute because we didn't want to hurt our mother's feelings.

We couldn't get over the change in Mom. Her stomach had deflated like a pricked balloon and she looked almost normal again.

And Aunt Sylvia had washed and waved her hair and Mom had powdered her nose and put a bit of lipstick on. She was sitting in the corner of the kitchen in the big rocking chair, with a baby in the crook of each arm. Uncle Phil had brought the rocking chair down from their house. Aunt Sylvia used to rock Ronnie to sleep in it every night, even when he was bigger than her. But of course they didn't need it anymore.

"What are their names?" asked Aunt Sylvia, hovering over them like a guardian angel.

"How about Tom for the little guy," suggested Robbie.

"How about Jim Junior," Jimmy said. He was serious!

"Stupid!" snapped Carrie and I.

"Melissa would suit the little girl," Aunt Sylvia said. "She's going to be pretty as a picture."

Carrie and I looked at the babies dubiously. I knew exactly what she was thinking. They both looked like yellow skinned rabbits to us.

"How about family names, like the rest of them," Dad said. We were all stuck with the names of dead ancestors.

Then Mom said, "Well, you can just relax because I've already chosen their names."

We all stopped talking to listen.

"Their names," Mom began rocking gently, "are Jay . . . " she looked adoringly at the tiny face in the blue blanket, "and Joy," she looked adoringly at the tiny face in the pink blanket.

"Sounds okay to me," Robbie said. "Well, I gotta go. I'm late for work." Robbie had a summer job at the Piggly Wiggly stuffing sausages.

"Okay by me, too," Jimmy said and ran out to play.

"Those are lovely names," approved Aunt Sylvia.

"That's settled then." Dad slapped his knee and went down to his workshop in the basement. He was making a double rocking horse: the kind with a flat horse on either side and a wide seat in the middle, big enough for two.

"Well, I must be going," Aunt Sylvia said. "You girls take good care of your mother and the babies. I'll let myself out. Bye bye."

Now Carrie and I and Mom were alone with the babies.

"Well, girls, what do you think?" Mom asked. "You haven't said much about my baby-twins."

We looked first at one and then the other. The one in blue was chewing his fist. The one in pink was sound asleep. Then we looked at each other; but we still didn't say anything.

"What is it? What's the matter? Is it their names? Don't you like them?"

"The names are okay," we said. "But . . . "

"But what?"

"Are you always going to call them your 'baby-twins'?"

Mom rolled her eyes at us. "Well, that's what they are," she said clucking her tongue. "My 'baby' twins. After all, you two are big girls now. And boy and girl twins are special."

Carrie and I wrinkled our noses and read each other's minds. "What does that make us?" we wondered.

Chapter 9

A Ruined Vacation

The twins took up every second of Mom's time — and ours.

"Where do you two think you're off to?" Mom would shout. Then, before we could escape, or answer, she'd say, "Can't you see I need some help here?"

This time, Mom pointed to a basket full of freshly washed diapers sitting in the middle of the kitchen floor. "Take that basket of laundry and hang it out on the line. Then come right back in."

We each grabbed a handle of the wicker basket and lugged it out the back door.

"I hope nobody sees us," I said, glancing over the fence.

"It wouldn't be so bad if it was ordinary laundry," Carrie said, pinning the first glistening white nappy (Mom's word for diaper) on the clothesline.

"Yeah," I agreed. "It's disgusting."

"It's worse than that. It's . . . it's . . . it's reprehensible," exploded Carrie.

"Yeah!" I agreed again. (Another word I'd have to look up.)

No sooner were all the diapers flapping in the breeze than Mom came out on the back stoop looking all dishevelled. "Can't you two hurry up? I'm swamped in here."

"Do you want us to do the grocery shopping, Mom?" At least that would get us out of the house. It was nearly noon and there was no sign of lunch.

"No," Mom said. "Robbie's picking up the groceries at the Piggly Wiggly before he comes home."

"Where's Jimmy?" we asked. The little brat had made himself scarce right after breakfast.

"I don't know," Mom said. "But at least he's out of my road."

"Well . . . what do you want us to do?"

"It's time the baby-twins were fed and I haven't even got the beds made yet," Mom said. "I've never been so behind in my work. So run upstairs and make them. And don't just throw them together. Make them properly."

We grunted with disgust and headed for the stairs.

"I heard that!" Mom called after us. "The least you can do is help willingly."

Jimmy's end of the boys' room was a mess. It looked as if it had been hit by a bomb; shorts and socks and comic books and gum wrappers and potato chips were scattered, like autumn leaves, all over the floor. We kicked everything under his bed and threw the covers up over his pillow.

Robbie's end of the room wasn't as bad. So we made his bed properly and propped his guitar case up against the wall.

Next we tiptoed into Mom and Dad's room and made

their bed carefully. In the corner of their room stood the giant crib that Uncle Phil had made especially for Ronnie. Uncle Phil had brought it over for the twins. They were just waking up from their morning nap.

"Cooo, cooo!" they said, mimicking the doves that sometimes perched outside the screen on the windowsill.

We leaned over the side of the crib and cooed back at them. They wiggled their tiny pink fingers and almost smiled.

"Oh, they're irresistible," Carrie cried as she reached in and picked Joy up.

"And soaking wet!" I cried, holding Jay at arm's length. "What'll we do?"

"We'll have to change them," Carrie said. "At least I don't smell 'the other.'"

So we changed them from the skin out and carried them down to Mom.

The minute she saw them her frown changed to a smile.

Their bottles were ready on the table. Mom sank with a sigh into the rocking chair which had been permanently installed in the corner of our big kitchen. We put a baby in each of her arms.

"Thank you, girls," she said. "You've been a big help this morning. Now make yourselves some lunch before you go out to play."

We made Mom lunch, too: banana and peanut-butter sandwich, spread real thick, and an apple for dessert.

* * *

The street was empty except for Molly, the Pools' black-and-white cat. She was slinking after a robin so we shooed her away.

Our friends on the street — the ones who didn't have babies in the family — had disappeared hours ago. Mostly the girls went window-shopping along Jefferson Avenue and the boys headed for the baseball diamond.

"What'll we do?" asked Carrie.

"Let's go to the schoolyard and see who's playing baseball," I suggested.

We both knew who we hoped to see: Hunter Davidson. But the schoolyard was empty except for Sandy Mason and his dog, Reg.

We liked Reg but we didn't like Sandy. Nobody liked Sandy. He was one of those kids who always smelled funny and had a runny nose.

He looked up expecting the usual rebuff. His glasses were broken and mended with tape. His sandy hair was matted with dirt. And his shirt was held together with a safety pin.

"How's Reg?" we said, for something to say.

Sandy looked surprised that we spoke to him. "He's okay, 'cept for his paw," he answered.

Reg was holding his right paw up off the ground. We dropped to our knees to look. It was cracked and red between the toes.

Just then our Jimmy rode into the schoolyard on his bicycle. "What's the matter with the dog?" he asked.

"He's got a sore paw," we said.

"Why don't you wash it at the water fountain?" he said. "Here, I got a clean hanky."

Sandy carried Reg, who was a small dog, to the fountain where we washed his paw and dried it with Jimmy's hanky.

"I see something shiny in there," Jimmy said.

Gently prying Reg's toes apart, we saw a straight pin lodged in the pink pad with only the pinhead visible.

"Hold his muzzle so he won't bite," I said to Sandy. "This might hurt."

I held the toes apart and Carrie nipped the pin out so quick Reg didn't even whimper. Instantly he began licking his paw.

"Gee, thanks," Sandy said.

"That's okay," we said. And Jimmy said, "See you around," and shoved off.

Carrie and I ran home to tell Mom all about it. She was rolling pie dough on the kitchen table.

"See how good it makes you feel when you help someone?" she said after hearing the story. "Now you know how I feel when you girls help me with the baby-twins."

Carrie and I gave each other a skeptical glance. "Let's go find Lorena and Nancy," we said and headed for the front door.

"Where are you off to this time?" Mom called after us. "The washing must be dry by now."

We groaned and retraced our steps to the backyard. Sure enough, the diapers were dry as paper. "Next time we escape . . . " Carrie said, yanking them off the line.

" . . . we won't hurry back," I finished.

* * *

That night Aunt Sylvia brought over a chicken casserole with crispy brown biscuit top. At the supper table Jimmy said, "Dad, guess what me and the twins did today?"

"What twins?" Dad asked.

"Carrie and Connie, of course," Jimmy said. "The baby-twins don't do nothing."

"Don't do anything," Carrie corrected.

"My babies can do lots of things," Mom said haughtily. "They can smile and coo . . . "

"And cry," Carrie and I added.

"They hardly ever cry," Mom snapped. "And they're already trying to roll over."

"Yep," Dad added. "I think they're the smartest kids we've had so far." He always implied that there might be more of us in the future, just to get Mom's goat.

But it went right over Mom's head this time. "I do think they are exceptional," she said. "Why, they're already making strange. Mrs. Mortimer came to see them today and when she leaned over to pick Jay up I could swear he gave her a dirty look."

Carrie and I glanced at each other. "Onion breath!" we mouthed.

Mom went on and on about the smartness of the babies until we all tuned her out. Jimmy forgot what he was going to tell Dad and Robbie went upstairs to strum on his guitar and Dad started reading the paper before he even finished his sago pudding. Carrie and I did the dishes without being asked.

* * *

Later, in the privacy of our bedroom with the door shut, I asked Carrie, "How do you really feel about the s?"

Carrie thought for a minute.

"Well?" I prompted.

"I'm vacillating," Carrie said.

"What the heck does that mean?" Sometimes I thought Carrie used big words just to get my goat. But I knew the real reason; ever since we were little, Carrie had been trying to "individuate." She always wanted to be different and I always wanted to stay the same. And one of her favourite ways of individuating was to use words I didn't know.

"Well, do you?" I asked again.

"Do I what?"

"Like the baby-twins."

"I guess so," she said. "But I'd like them better if they were in somebody else's family."

Just then we heard Mom and Dad coming up the stairs talking.

"I'm glad we decided to have a second family," we heard Mom say. "Now that Jimmy's half grown, I was missing having little ones around the house."

"Well, then . . . " We recognized the teasing note in our Dad's voice. "We can't let that happen again, now can we?"

Mom laughed as they went into their bedroom and shut the door.

"He can't be serious," Carrie said in a horrified whisper.

"If he was," I whispered back, "I don't think Mom would be laughing."

Chapter 10

Marilyn's Plans

Something happened at the end of August that arrested our jealousy of the babies. We had to admit that's what it was — jealousy. Robbie was very fond of them — almost fatherly, Dad remarked, for a seventeen-year-old boy. And Jimmy took them entirely for granted, which was strange since he had been the baby of the family for over ten years and it would be more natural for him to be jealous.

Anyway, one night we were all sitting around the supper table when the phone rang.

"Let it ring," Dad said. He hated the phone to interrupt his supper.

Mom just rolled her eyes and reached for the phone.

"Hello," she said. Then she covered the mouthpiece and told Dad, "It's Sylvia." As she listened her eyes got bigger and bigger. She kept saying, "Really! Oh, *really.* That's wonderful news."

When she hung up she clapped her hands together and cried, "Guess what?" Before we could guess, she told

41

us. "Marilyn has just announced her engagement to her boyfriend and she wants Carrie and Connie to be her bridesmaids."

We could hardly believe our ears. Marilyn didn't even like us very much — which was another case of jealousy. Her mother and father were very fond of us twins and Marilyn knew it. So she had good reason to be jealous.

But the day she came with her mother to show us her ring, a solitary diamond set in white gold, she suddenly changed her tune.

"You're like sisters to me," she gushed, giving us an unexpected hug. "You just *have* to be my bridesmaids."

She even let us help with the invitations. Sitting around their kitchen table Marilyn addressed the parchment envelopes in her pretty handwriting and we stuffed and sealed them and licked the stamps.

I read the embossed invitations over and over: "Mr. and Mrs. Phillip Conway request the honour of your presence at the marriage of their only daughter, Marilyn Jean, to Private Darrell Andrew Miller (United States Marine Corps) on Saturday, October 15, 1955 . . . "

"I really wanted a spring wedding," Marilyn explained, her voice lilting with excitement. "But now that Darrell has been posted overseas on a year's tour of duty he wants me to go with him."

"How romantic!" Carrie and I swooned at the news. But when we saw the pained look on Aunt Sylvia's face we stopped.

* * *

One night Mom said, "I think we should have a 'street shower' for Marilyn. We're the only family she's got, and I'm sure the neighbors would all love to come."

42

"Don't go biting off more than you can chew," Dad said. "You've got your hands full these days."

"But the babies are so good now," Mom protested. "They don't get up for their night bottle until eleven o'clock so that'll give me plenty of time. And I'm sure the twins will pitch in and help, won't you girls?"

Hearing her calling us "the twins" again made us game for anything. "Sure," we said. "What do you want us to do?"

"Well, for one thing, you can write out the invitations — you should be in good practice by now. And you can deliver them by hand to the whole neighborhood."

The next day we went down to the five-and-dime store and bought bridal shower cards and streamers and bows. That night Jimmy had to do the dishes because we were too busy writing the invitations.

"I hate doing dishes," crabbed Jimmy, up to his elbows in Lux.

"You like to eat, don't you?" snapped Dad.

"Sure." Jimmy stopped clattering the dishes into the tray. "What have you got?"

"Do a good job and I'll reward you with two ginger snaps," Dad said. "Maybe three."

"Yuck!" Jimmy slapped a saucepan into the water like a beaver slapping its tail in a pond. "I hate ginger snaps."

Of course Dad already knew that. "Too bad," he grinned. "All the more for me."

We wrote out thirty-nine invitations and hand-delivered them the next day.

Mrs. Mortimer must have caught the envelope as it went sliding through the letter slot because the door flew open before we could make our getaway.

"What's this, then?" she cried, ripping open the envelope. "Oh, my, isn't that lovely. Tell your poor mother I'll be there with bells on!"

We leaped down the veranda steps and hurried next door.

"Poor mother!" I snorted.

"Bells on!" Carrie sniffed.

"I think she's got bells in her belfry," I said.

"Isn't that supposed to be bats?" laughed Carrie.

"Whatever," I said.

*　*　*

An hour later we came home empty-handed.

"Did you get them all delivered?" Mom asked.

"Sure, and quite a few people opened them and said they were coming."

"Do we have to buy Marilyn a present out of our own money, Mom?" I asked.

"Of course," Mom said.

"Who else's?" Dad said.

So we went upstairs to count our money. I had five dollars saved up. Carrie had four dollars and fifty cents. We could buy a nice present and have lots left over.

"I've got an idea," I said. "Let's buy her a dishpan."

"And a matching drainboard," Carrie said. "Can't you just see Marilyn doing dishes?"

"I get the picture," I said. And we both screamed laughing.

*　*　*

The bridal shower was more fun than a picnic. All the ladies in the neighbourhood came, overflowing our living room and dining room. Everybody was talking at once. It was like being in the middle of a beehive. Mom put Jimmy out on the veranda to stand guard. As soon as he spotted Aunt Sylvia's Chevrolet coming up the street he hollered through the screen door, "HERE THEY COME!"

Mom clapped her hands, but nobody heard. So Dad put two fingers in his mouth and blew an ear-splitting whistle that shocked everybody into silence. Carrie and I switched the lights off. Mom stepped out into the hall and shut the French doors behind her.

It was so quiet I could hear Mrs. Mortimer's chest rattling. She was a heavy smoker. Then I heard the babies crying in the distance. "I hope we don't have to mind them," I whispered.

"No. I heard Mom tell Dad it was his turn," Carrie whispered back.

Suddenly the French doors flew open and we snapped the lights back on and everybody hollered: "SURPRISE!"

Marilyn squealed and her cheeks flushed almost as red as her hair.

Taking her hands, Carrie and I led her to the bridal chair and sat her down under a waterfall of crepe-paper streamers.

The presents were piled high around Marilyn's feet. As she opened them she handed Carrie the ribbons and bows. Carrie made a colourful hat out of a paper plate. My job was to read the cards. Marilyn cried out in genuine delight at every present: she got pots and pans and Pyrex pie plates. Tea towels and dishcloths and fancy cups and saucers. Tea kettles and gravy boats and salt-and-pepper shakers. Cream jugs and sugar bowls and napkin rings. The very last present — Carrie's and mine

— was the biggest. Marilyn ripped off the bridal paper revealing the dish-pan and drainboard.

At first Marilyn was speechless. Then, giving us each a haughty look, she said, "Thank you very much, it's just what I needed." Then she added, "And I'll remember it when your turn comes around."

Carrie and I frowned at each other. "Are you thinking what I'm thinking?" I whispered.

"Exactly," she whispered back.

* * *

We helped Aunt Sylvia and Mom serve the refreshments: sandwiches with the crusts cut off and pickles and olives and crackers and cheese. And a mock wedding cake with clouds of white icing and a bride and groom on top.

"I made it myself from scratch," Mom boasted.

"Oh, Auntie!" Marilyn clapped her hands in delight. "When did you have the time?"

"Oh, I whipped it up while the babies were having their nap," Mom bragged. "They were good as gold today, so it was no trouble at all."

Mrs. Mortimer polished off two platefuls of sandwiches. When I offered her a square of the beautiful cake, she patted her chest, gave a loud burp, and declared, "I couldn't eat another bite."

I was just about to whisk them away when she reached out and snatched two big pieces. "But I'll take some home," she cried.

All in all, the shower was a huge success.

Chapter 11

Eighth Grade

It was a relief to go back to school. We loved eighth grade from the very first day. It was swell being the oldest kids in junior high. It made us feel quite grown up. And it took our minds off Marilyn's wedding for a change.

"Let's dress alike," Carrie said on the first morning.

"Okay," I agreed. "And part our hair down the middle."

For some reason we couldn't explain, looking exactly alike gave us a strange sense of security. And it also got us lots of attention. Especially from boys.

The first day was orientation. The teacher in charge took one look at Carrie and me, blinked, and immediately assigned us to different classrooms. Carrie's homeroom was 203 and mine was 223. Her homeroom teacher was Mr. Krowe and mine was Miss Proud.

We didn't see each other again until lunchtime in the cafeteria. Mom had given us twenty-five cents each to buy our lunch the first day. "But from now on," she said, "you'll have to make your own lunches every night

47

because I won't have time to do it with two families." We hated that — being divided into two families.

On the way home we had lots to tell each other.

"I think I've made a new friend already," I said.

"What's his name?" teased Carrie.

"Not him, smarty!" I gave her a shove. "Her. Her name's Barbara Hastings. And you know something?"

"I do know something." Carrie laughed and tossed her shiny hair over her shoulder. "After all, I'm almost in high school."

"If you're going to act goofy I'm not going to tell you anything."

"Sorry. I'm listening."

"Well, Barbara's birthday is the very same day as ours, May 16. And you should have seen her face when I told her I had an identical twin. She can't wait to meet you."

Turning up our front walk we raced each other up the steps.

The twin pram (Mom called the baby carriage "the pram" because she was English) was in the corner of the veranda. We crept over and peaked inside. Both Jay and Joy were sound asleep, their tiny faces turned to each other. They didn't look anything like skinned rabbits anymore. They had dimples on their hands and their cheeks were pink.

"Aww," we said. Then we rushed in the house, letting the screen door slam behind us. The twins woke up screaming and Mom came racing down the hall mad as a hatter.

"Well, thanks a heap!" she snapped at us sarcastically. "I just got them nicely to sleep." She bumped the pram up into the front hall. "Now you'll have to help me get the supper. Go upstairs and change out of your school clothes. The last thing I need is extra laundry."

Glumly we went upstairs, changed, and came back down to the kitchen. Jimmy was halfway inside the fridge.

"What are you doing?" I gave him a poke.

"Hunting," came the muffled reply.

"Well, you won't find any big game in there," Carrie said.

Jimmy backed out with a quart of milk and a wiener. "Where's Robbie?" he asked.

"How should we know?" we snapped. "Get out of our way."

"It would be my pleasure," he said, perfectly mimicking Uncle Phil, who was known for his gentlemanly manners. Then he poured himself a tumbler of milk, bit the end off the wiener, breezed into the living room and turned on the television to watch *Howdy Doody*.

* * *

Everybody was quiet around the supper table, waiting for Mom to get over her mad. Dad, who was afraid of no man, as he often told us, had taken to pussyfooting around Mom since the arrival of the new babies. He liked bread with his dinner but instead of asking for it he just stood up and got it himself.

After we ate the supper of leftovers that we had helped Mom throw together, Jimmy asked, "What's for dessert?"

"DESSERT! DESSERT!" Mom screeched. (You'd think he'd said a bad word). "I was going to make floating island until the girls woke the babies by slamming the screen door on purpose."

"On purpose!" cried Carrie.

"It was an accident," I explained.

"Accident or not, it makes no difference if it wakes the baby-twins." Mom was on the verge of tears.

"Now, now," Dad said in a placating voice.

"Don't 'now, now,' me," she snapped.

"How be I get a brick of ice cream?" offered Robbie.

"Good idea, Rob." Dad tipped his chair back on its hind legs and fished a dollar bill out of his pocket. "Get two bricks."

While we waited for Robbie to come back with the ice cream, Carrie and I cleared the table and Mom made the tea. I couldn't help but notice how bedraggled Mom looked. Before the babies were born she had always made a point of putting on a clean housedress and fixing her hair before Dad came home. He was so proud of her black wavy hair. But today it was a mess and her housedress (the same one she had had on that morning) was all wrinkled and splotched with baby spit-up.

"Well, girls," Dad said tiredly. "How was your day?" The way he said it sounded like an afterthought.

Just as we opened our mouths to answer, Jimmy reached for the milk pitcher, the one shaped like a cow, and knocked it over. It landed with a crash on the edge of his plate. The milk splashed all over the table and the cow's tail broke off. The noise started the babies crying again. They were still in their pram by the kitchen door.

"Now look what you've done!" Mom jumped up, grabbed the dishcloth from the sink and began furiously mopping up the mess.

Jimmy, who wasn't used to being snapped at, pouted like a baby. Dad got up and pulled the pram over by his chair and jiggled it with his foot until the crying gradually stopped.

When Robbie returned, we ate our ice cream and drank our tea in silence.

Draining her cup, Mom heaved a big sigh. Then she turned to us and her round blue eyes were pooled with tears. "I'm sorry, girls," she said. "I'm just not myself lately."

"It's okay, Mom," we said. Then we cleared the table, did the dishes, and went into the living room. *The Lone Ranger*, Jimmy's favourite program, was just coming on. The next program was an old Roy Rogers movie and the screen had gone all snowy so it was not worth watching. We got bored and went to bed leaving Mom and Dad dozing in their chairs.

Lying on my back, staring up at the ceiling, I said to Carrie, "Have you noticed that Mom mostly calls us 'the girls' now instead of 'the twins'?"

"Yes," she answered. "I used to hate always being the twins. Especially when she called us her 'twinny-twin-twins.' But now I sort of miss it."

"Me, too. Maybe when the babies get older she'll have more time for the rest of us again."

"Well, don't hold your breath," grumbled Carrie, rolling over in her bunk.

Just then we heard Robbie playing "Rock-a-bye-baby" on his guitar. Carrie and I started singing softly, "Rock-a-bye-baby, on the treetop, when the wind blows, the cradle will rock; when the bough breaks, the cradle will fall. Down tumbles baby, cradle and all."

"I hope that's not wishful thinking," Carrie whispered.

"Don't say that!" I whispered back.

The next tune he played was a sad refrain we didn't know. But it suited our mood and lulled us off to sleep.

Chapter 12

Wedding Plans

The excitement of the wedding plans filled our lives for weeks. Aunt Sylvia and Marilyn took us downtown to the Bridal Shoppe where Marilyn's wedding gown was being made and had us measured for our bridesmaids' dresses.

"I'd like mine in pink," Carrie said. That's where we differentiated. Carrie's favourite colour was red and mine was green. Of course she knew a bridesmaid couldn't wear red, so she was willing to settle for pink.

"I'd like mine in green," I said, as the lady circled my waist with the measuring tape.

"Well, you're both getting mauve," Marilyn said. "Mauve will set off my white chiffon to perfection."

"*Mauve!*" we both yelled at once. "Isn't mauve purple?"

"Mauve is mauve, you silly twits," snapped Marilyn.

"Mauve is our most unfavourite colour," we objected.

"Well, I'm the bride and it's my choice," said Marilyn.

We looked at Aunt Sylvia but she just raised her pencilled eyebrows and shrugged.

When we got home we asked our mom.

"Marilyn's right," Mom said. "It's her choice. So don't say a word if you want to be her bridesmaids."

We did want to be Marilyn's bridesmaids because it would be thrilling and our girlfriends would all be sick with envy. So we took our mother's advice and didn't say a word.

Marilyn's fiancé, Darrell, had asked Robbie to be his best man because he didn't have a brother and all his cousins were girls, and his best friend, another Marine, had been posted to California.

"The expense is going to put us in the poorhouse," Mom complained. She was at the stove stirring the baby-twins' formula. "The girls' dresses are going to cost a small fortune. And Robbie will need a brand-new suit if he's going to be best man."

Taking the pot of milk off the stove, Mom began pouring it into the sterilized bottles lined up like glass soldiers along the kitchen counter.

"Oh, don't worry your head," Dad said, jiggling a fussy baby in the crook of each arm. "Phil and Sylvia have been mighty good to us. So we'll manage somehow."

* * *

One Sunday Robbie said, out of a clear blue sky, "Do you two know how to dance?"

Dance! "Why do we need to know?" we asked.

"Just in case somebody asks you," Robbie said.

"There's going to be dancing?"

"Well, sure. There always is at a wedding. Where have you been all your life?"

We had never been to a wedding so it was news to us.

"What'll we do?" we groaned.

"I'll teach you if you like," Robbie said in an offhand way.

Carrie and I raised our eyebrows at each other. Robbie usually went out of his way not to even touch us by accident, and here he was offering to show us how to dance.

Mom and Dad had been listening in the background. "Wonders never cease," we heard Mom say.

Dad was so pleased at Robbie's unexpected thoughtfulness that he rolled up the living-room rug and put a dance record on the turntable. It was Frank Sinatra crooning a love song.

Standing about a foot away, Robbie took my right hand and placed my left hand on his shoulder. Then he put his other hand gingerly on my back. "We'll start with the two-step," he said. "One, two, three . . . one, two, three . . . " I tripped over his feet.

"Just relax," he said giving my arm a shake. "You're stiff as a mop handle."

"Well, you said it was a two-step," I complained. "And you keep counting to three."

Carrie caught on quicker than I did so we practiced in our room at night and by the end of the week Robbie said, "I think you've got it."

"Now show me, Rob!" demanded Jimmy. "Some girl might ask me to dance."

"Fat chance!" laughed Robbie. "That'll be the day you catch me dancing with a guy. But don't worry, Sport, nobody's going to ask you."

Well, that made Jimmy howl and Carrie and I went into hysterics and suddenly Mom poked her head between the French doors. "Shush!" she hissed. "You'll wake the babies. And whoever wakes them has to mind them."

We all shut up like clams.

Chapter 13

Wedding Bells

The big day finally arrived, and to our relief the mauve dresses that Marilyn had insisted on were absolutely beautiful. They were the colour of violets and we each carried a nosegay of pink rosebuds and white baby's breath.

Marilyn was the perfect bride in white satin and fluffy white chiffon and a bridal bouquet of glorious fall flowers. And Aunt Sylvia was the typical beaming mother of the bride.

It was a small wedding, with only about fifty people there, because both the bride's and groom's families were small. The ceremony was held in the little white frame church on Jefferson Avenue where Marilyn and Ronnie had been christened.

The service was sweet and simple and when the minister pronounced them man and wife and Darrell gently lifted Marilyn's veil and gave her her first marital kiss, a collective sigh drifted like mist over the congregation. I glanced at Aunt Sylvia and was surprised to see two tears wending their way down her pink cheeks. And Uncle Phil had his arm around her.

Then the married couple tripped happily down the aisle and Carrie and I went tripping after them.

We lined up on the church steps under a bright blue sky for photographs; then we gathered under the huge maple tree on the church lawn, our feet buried in red and gold leaves, for more pictures.

Then the bride did something completely unexpected: she left her new husband's side and, picking up her long train with one hand, her bridal bouquet in the other, she went through the small wooden gate into the little church cemetery.

Only her mother and father followed her. Everyone else stayed outside the white picket fence and watched as she laid her bridal bouquet, lovingly, on her brother Ronnie's grave.

* * *

The wedding reception was held at the American Legion Hall just around the corner from the church. Uncle Phil was a proud veteran of World War II. He had served in the Army overseas and had been awarded the Purple Heart. The Legion Hall was decorated with white streamers and paper wedding bells and pink carnations on every table.

We sat at the head table with the bride and groom because we were part of the wedding party. Robbie looked amazingly handsome (for a brother) in his blue serge suit and white shirt and blue tie.

After the wedding feast Darrell and Marilyn cut the two-tiered wedding cake. Then, in her sweetest bridey voice, Marilyn said, "How would you twins like to help me serve?" So we did and that was fun and lots of people told us how lovely we looked in our mauve dresses.

Afterwards, when the tables were cleared away, a baby grand piano was uncovered and a man I didn't know began to play. The first piece he played was "Daddy's Little Girl" and Uncle Phil, the father of the bride, danced with his little girl. There wasn't a dry eye in the Legion Hall.

Then, when the dancing began in earnest, Carrie and I became suddenly shy and we backed up against the wall. A sweet lady with bluish-white hair, who could have been Marilyn's grandmother but wasn't, came over to us and said, "You girls look like adorable twin dolls. Now stay right where you are. I want my hubby to take your picture."

She scurried across the hall, dodging between the dancers, and came hurrying back dragging a man, bald as an egg, by the hand.

"There now, Sam, what did I tell you? Aren't they pretty as a picture?"

"I'll go you one better, Mildred," he said, giving us a false-tooth grin. "They're visions of feminine pulchritude."

"What does that mean?" I whispered to Carrie.

"I don't know, but I'm sure it's a compliment," she whispered back.

So we smiled and posed and the flashbulbs popped, catching everybody's eye. For a few minutes we were the centre of attention.

The flashes attracted the bride and groom and they came waltzing over to see what was going on. Marilyn smiled at the egg-headed man and he promptly forgot us and turned the camera on her. But we didn't care because right after that the boys started lining up to dance with us.

* * *

We had a terrible time getting to sleep that night. And the next morning Carrie woke up sighing.

"I had the most marvelous dream," she said.

"Me, too," I said. "What did you dream?"

"I dreamed I was the bride and you were my bridesmaid."

"Me, too!" We often had the same dream. "Only I was the bride and you were my bridesmaid."

"Who was the groom in your dream?" she asked suspiciously.

"Hunter Davidson, who else?"

"Oh," she snapped in disgust. "You can't even make up your own dream!"

What she said didn't make any sense but I knew exactly what she meant.

Chapter 14

The House of Beauty

Every day on our way to and from junior high we passed Aunt Sylvia's hairdressing parlour. It was on Jefferson Avenue and it was called The House of Beauty. Now that she had no children at home, Aunt Sylvia seemed to be working day and night.

We always stopped and waved through the plate glass window. If she wasn't too busy she'd beckon us to come in. If she had time she'd even fix our hair. If business picked up while we were there, she'd ask us to lend a hand.

"You're just in the nick of time," she said breathlessly when we stopped in to get out of the wind. It was the middle of November and all the leaves had blown off the trees, but it hadn't snowed yet. "I'm run off my feet today." Aunt Sylvia twisted a lady's blonde hair into pink permanent-wave curlers. "I haven't even had a chance to sweep up." Hair was spread, like a fluffy carpet, all over the linoleum floor.

"I'll do it for you, Aunt Sylvia," I volunteered.

"Oh, thank you, dear. You'll find the broom and dustpan in the closet."

"What can I do, Aunt Sylvia?" asked Carrie.

"How would you like to give Mrs. Mack a shampoo? My shampoo girl phoned in sick today."

We threw down our books on a swivel chair. Then Carrie ran to the back of the shop where the sinks and dryers were and I got the broom out of the closet.

Curls of many colours were scattered everywhere: white and red and black and brown and blonde and even purple. It gave me a creepy feeling, gathering all those dead curls into a pile. I swept them up as quickly as I could and dumped them into the trash can.

When we were finished our jobs we asked if there was anything else we could do.

"Well . . . " Aunt Sylvia was covering the permanent-wave lady's head in a clear plastic bag. Three more customers — clients, Aunt Sylvia called them — were sitting along the bench in front of the window, leafing impatiently through movie magazines. "If you have time . . . but maybe you should give your mother a call to see if she needs you."

"She doesn't need us," we said. "We just get on her nerves."

One of the ladies on the bench stared at us over her magazine. "Do they always talk together like that?" she asked, giving us a queer look.

"Always," laughed Aunt Sylvia. "All right, then," she said to us. "You can do whatever you like."

So Carrie shampooed the ladies one by one and I tidied up the magazines and polished the mirrors and swept up more dead curls.

We were having so much fun that we lost all track of time. It was seven o'clock when the phone rang.

"Get that for me, Connie," Aunt Sylvia said. "It's probably your Uncle Phil wondering why I'm so late."

But it wasn't Uncle Phil, it was our mom. "What are you doing down there at this hour?" she shrieked so loudly over the phone everybody in the place could hear. "Why didn't you come straight home? Are you both there? Which one am I talking to? Your supper's cold and your father's fit to be tied and I'm nearly out of my mind with worry."

"Okay, Mom. It's me, Connie. We're coming!"

Aunt Sylvia looked mortified. "Oh, dear! Tell your mother I'm sorry for keeping you," she said. "Help yourselves to five dollars out of the till — I insist — and hurry home."

Robbie had been sent to meet us because it was pitch dark. "Idiots!" he yelled, riding his bike behind us. "Morons. I hope Dad belts the daylights out of the two of you."

But he didn't. He just ordered us to bed without our supper. As we passed the French doors we glanced into the living room. Mom was sitting on the sofa, a baby in each arm.

"Goodnight, Mom," we said.

She didn't even look up. Our feet dragged as we went up the stairs. We hid our five-dollar bill in the back of our clothes-closet shelf where Jimmy wouldn't find it. We had caught him rummaging through our dresser drawers once but he hadn't stolen anything. He was just sleuthing, he said, hunting for clues. He was going to be a Private Eye when he grew up and he needed the practice.

We got our PJs on and I went to the bathroom for a glass of water. Then we opened our school books on the twin-sized desk that Dad had made us.

"Have you got a candy bar in your school bag?" Carrie asked, rubbing her flat stomach.

"No. I wish I had. I'm so hungry I could eat a toad."

Just then we saw our doorknob twisting slowly. The door creaked open a crack.

"Oh, no!" we whispered, expecting Dad.

But it wasn't Dad, it was Jimmy, his dark curly head peering around the door. "Here." He thrust in a brown paper sack. "Take it quick before I get caught."

"Thanks, Jimmy," we said. "We owe you one."

He shut the door quietly and we ripped open the sack. A delicious smell seeped up our noses. Inside were two incredibly messy peanut-butter and jelly sandwiches. We fell on them like hungry dogs and demolished them in two minutes flat. Then we licked our fingers clean and washed the sticky mess down with water.

A few minutes later the door creaked open again. This time it was Robbie. He didn't say a word. He just threw in a white paper bag and shut the door. The bag landed on our bedroom mat and we pounced on it like starving cats on a mouse.

Jelly beans! Red and purple jelly beans. Carrie crept to the bathroom for more water and I divided the candies into two piles: ten red and ten purple. Carrie liked the red ones best.

"You know what?" she said, licking her lips with a red tongue.

"What?" I said.

"I think this is what Mom means when she says 'Don't

pay it back, pass it on.'"

"Yeah," I said. "Remember last year on Halloween? Jimmy had a sore throat and couldn't go trick-or-treating so we took an extra bag and got it filled for him?"

"Right," said Carrie. "And just yesterday we saved the last piece of lemon pie for Robbie before Jimmy had a chance to gobble it up."

"I just thought of something else, too," I said. "Remember Mom telling us that her Grandma Conroy, the one I'm named after, always said passing a favour on was like forging a love-chain?"

"Yeah. But I don't think Robbie and Jimmy love us," said Carrie.

"Maybe they do," I said. "In their own goofy way." I tossed my last jelly bean up in the air and caught it on my tongue. It went sliding down before I got a chance to taste it.

We laughed, then, and went to bed.

"I feel vindicated," said Carrie from the bottom bunk.

"Exactly," I said.

Chapter 15

The Christmas Play

Mom said we were not allowed to stop at The House of Beauty anymore. Ever. We could only wave to Aunt Sylvia as we went by. Luckily, the Christmas play came along and took our minds off everything else.

It was an original script written by our English teacher, Miss Nonnie Paddison. It was called "Christmas Family Reunion." Carrie and I were chosen to play the twin sisters who were in love with the same boy.

"How ironic," I said.

"Satirical," Carrie said.

We had been in Miss Paddison's English class from the very first day, and every time she saw us she literally gasped. "Mirror twins!" she'd exclaim, shaking her head. "Fascinating."

"And when you look at me with those four gold-speckled green eyes I fairly get shivers up my spine," she added, when she called us in after school to tell us about the play.

We darted each other a weird glance. Nobody had

ever said that to us before. But the next thing she said mollified us.

"I wrote the play especially for you two," she gushed. Miss Paddison was a real gusher and sometimes, when she got excited, she even sprayed. She gave us the script to take home and study. "There are two boys I have in mind for the male lead — Hunter Davidson or Dale Moran."

"Who's Dale Moran?" We'd never heard that name before.

"He's a new boy from Fort Wayne, Indiana," Miss Paddison explained. "And I can't decide which one best suits the part of Blake Summerside. So I want you to read it over and let me know what you think."

Hunter ran to catch up to us on the way home. "Has Miss Paddison picked the leading man yet?" he asked anxiously.

"She hasn't decided. She wants our opinion first," I said.

"And we haven't made up our minds yet," teased Carrie.

"Ah, c'mon, gimme a break. Just think ten years from now, when I'm a big Hollywood heartthrob, you can say you knew me when."

We had already made up our minds, of course, but we decided to keep him in suspense.

That night we rehearsed our lines. The twins in the play were named Gillian and Jennifer. And Gillian got the man in the end. We both wanted to be Gillian, of course, so we flipped a coin and Carrie won. I thought I'd die of envy . . . until the next day when I met Dale Moran.

Jason Gallagher paled by comparison. If possible, Dale was even handsomer than Hunter Davidson. He had big brown eyes, slick black hair, and white even teeth like Chiclets, that sparkled when he smiled.

Miss Paddison made the costumes herself and Carrie and I were thrilled with ours. The dresses were green velvet with big skirts and lace collars (like Scarlett O'Hara's in *Gone With the Wind*, only they weren't made out of curtains) and red velvet bows to hold back our naturally wavy brown hair.

"I think I'm in love," I told Carrie while we were trying on our costumes.

"With which one?"

"Both."

"Well, don't hold your breath," she said, "Mom and Dad won't even let us start dating until we're sixteen."

But it was exciting, just the same, being in a play with all that masculine pulchritude.

* * *

We were late getting home every night after rehearsal so Mom sent Robbie to meet us because it was dark.

"Who did Miss Paddison pick for leading man?" asked Robbie, pushing his bike through the snow.

"Hunter Davidson," I said. "But I think Dale Moran's got the best part. He's the long-lost brother . . . "

" . . . who turns up on the doorstep on Christmas Eve," continued Carrie. "And Mr. Egbert, the school janitor, has built a real doorstep and a gas lamp on to the set outside the house so the audience sees the long-lost brother before the family does."

"Are you coming to opening night?" we asked Robbie as we kicked our snowy boots off in the front hall.

"If I've got nothing better to do," he said, shrugging off his windbreaker.

We knew what he meant. He and Betty Pool, the girl next door, were going steady now, much to Mom's consternation.

"WE'LL ALL BE THERE!" Mom shouted from the kitchen.

"I MIGHT BE BUSY!" Robbie shouted back.

"No you won't," Mom said.

"Can I come, too?" called Jimmy through the French doors.

"Of course, dopey. You heard Mom — you've got no choice," we said.

* * *

The play was on for three nights running and our whole family came on opening night. Dad was supposed to be working the night shift but he got his friend at the Ford Motor Company to trade shifts with him. "I wouldn't miss it for all the tea in China," he said as he helped Mom into her good coat with the lamb's-wool collar.

With her hand on the doorknob, Carrie asked, "Are Aunt Sylvia and Uncle Phil coming with us?"

"Or are they going to mind the baby-twins tonight?" I asked. I tried not to call them that but it slipped out again.

"Mrs. Mortimer is coming to watch them," Mom answered curtly.

"Why?" we asked. Aunt Sylvia always watched the babies.

"Why not?" snapped Mom.

"Mrs. Mortimer's such a nosy parker," we said.

"And she's an old windbag," Jimmy added, making a rude noise from his rear end to prove his point.

"Har! Har! Har!" roared Robbie.

"Be quiet," Dad hissed. "Here she is now."

"Hello Mrs. Mortimer," we chimed as she stepped in the front door. "Goodbye Mrs. Mortimer."

Dad had parked Flash Gordon at the curb so we all piled in.

The play was a smash hit and Carrie and I and Hunter and Dale got three curtain calls.

* * *

On the day of the last performance, on the way home from school, we both got the same idea. "Let's stop at The House of Beauty and ask Aunt Sylvia to come," we said. What with the play and everything it seemed like weeks since we had talked to her.

She was so glad to see us she threw curlers in the air and ran to us with open arms.

"You've got to come to our school play, Aunt Sylvia," we cried, breathlessly, because she was hugging us so hard. "This is the last night and we've got leading roles and it's a smash hit."

"Ohhh . . . " she sighed. "How I wish I could."

"Couldn't you just close early for once? Please, please, Aunt Sylvia," we begged.

"Of course I could. It's not that. It's . . . it's your mother."

"Our mother!" We had been so busy with the play we hadn't really noticed anything wrong.

"She's still mad at me." Aunt Sylvia said with a pout.

"Oh, heck no," we said. "Not really." Mom and Aunt Sylvia had been best friends ever since we could remember. Mom could never stay mad at her "Sissy" for very

70

long. That's what they called each other because they had no sisters of their own.

"Yes, really." Aunt Sylvia bit her lip. "She doesn't answer the phone and I haven't seen the baby-twins for weeks on end." Aunt Sylvia was crazy about Jay and Joy. "How are the darlings?"

"They're getting awful cute," I had to admit.

"And big!" Carrie added. "Mom took them to Dr. Duncan yesterday and Jay weighs fifteen pounds and Joy weighs thirteen."

"You don't say?" cried Aunt Sylvia. Then a lady with wet hair let out a disgusted grunt and Aunt Sylvia hurried back to her.

At the door Carrie turned around. "Why don't you and Uncle Phil come?" she said, "Then drop in at our house afterwards . . . sort of unexpected."

"Oh, please, Aunt Sylvia," I begged. "It's the last performance."

Aunt Sylvia paused for a long moment. "Will your parents be there tonight?" she asked.

"No. Dad's on night shift and Mom's got the babies."

"That settles it," she said, "We'll come!"

* * *

From backstage, we could tell the auditorium was filling up from the scraping of chairs and the shuffling and laughing and talking.

We kept peeking through the curtains until at last we saw Aunt Sylvia and Uncle Phil, in the middle row.

"We have to do our very best tonight," we said.

And we did.

When the curtain rose for the last time the whole cast received foot-stomping applause and a standing ovation.

Then the principal presented Miss Paddison with a bouquet of red roses.

Mom had arranged for Miss Paddison to bring us home, but we introduced her to our aunt and uncle and explained that they would be taking us.

"Are you sure this is a good idea, Syl?" Uncle Phil asked as he pulled the Chevy up in front of our house on Newport Street.

"Yes," answered Aunt Sylvia decisively.

From the veranda we could see the flickering light of the television set through the living-room curtains. Dad and Jimmy were watching *What's My Line?* When he heard us, Dad came through the French doors. "She's up there," he said, nodding towards the stairs.

"Mom! Mom!" Carrie and I yelled up the stairs. "We're home and look who's with us!"

"Who?" Mom appeared at the top of the stairs, a blue-sleepered baby in one arm and a pink-sleepered baby in the other.

With a little cry, Aunt Sylvia dropped her handbag on the floor, spilling out her lipstick and compact, and sprinted up the stairs.

"Oh, the darlings!" she cried as she gathered the babies into her arms. Turning, she carried them down, step by step, ever so carefully, as if they were made of glass.

"Oh, Phil," she cried. She really cried. Tears were glistening on her false eyelashes. "Look at them. Did you ever see anything so gorgeous?"

Carrie and I watched as they went absolutely berserk over the baby-twins.

"Honestly." Carrie frowned. "They aren't that gorgeous."

I was just about to agree with her when I looked up and caught sight of my mother's face. She was positively beaming. She came down the stairs and threw her arms around her friend's shoulders.

"Oh, Sissy, I love you," she said.

"I love you, too, Sissy," said Aunt Sylvia.

Nudging Carrie, I said, "I've got a feeling Christmas is going to be superb this year."

"Indubitably," she agreed.

"Oh, for Pete's sake!" I said.

Chapter 16

Christmas Eve, 1955

On Christmas Eve, after hours of pleading, we finally got Mom's permission to go skating with Hunter Davidson and Dale Moran.

They were waiting for us on the sidewalk.

"Be sure you're home here by nine o'clock sharp!" Mom shouted from the front door, clutching her sweater-coat at her throat.

"We will," we hollered back as we ran down the street with the boys to the neighborhood ice rink.

The rink was crowded already and we had to wait our turn to sit on the bench and put on our skates. Dale and Hunter got theirs on in a jiffy. Then they helped us with ours. Dale laced mine up too tight but I didn't dare complain.

Dale was a super skater; we crossed arms, clasped hands and whirled around the circumference of the rink, avoiding the crowds in the middle. We never once changed partners. Every time Hunter and Carrie whizzed by we hollered at them without unclasping our hands. I saw Lorena and Nancy skating together so I tried to get their attention. But they stuck up their chins and turned their heads the other way. Then I saw Jason Gallagher go skating by with a girl I didn't know. I hoped he saw me. The rest of the crowd was a complete blur.

We lost all track of time until we saw Jimmy hanging over the boards waving frantically. "Connie! Carrie! Mom says come home right now!" he yelled. Then he added, "And Dad's mad!"

"Oh, no," we worried as we scrambled for a place on the bench to take off our skates. "If Dad's mad, it'll spoil Christmas."

But he wasn't. He just said, "Since when did nine o'clock mean nine-thirty?"

"Sorry, Daddy," we said.

Mom was in the living room peering critically up at the tree. "We need some new decorations," she said.

"No, we don't," Carrie and I protested. We loved all the old ornaments that reminded us of our childhood: flaky glass balls and faded lightbulbs and rusty ropes of tinsel. Dad had even offered to buy a new star for the top, but we cherished the tarnished silver one he'd made us years ago out of cardboard and silver paper from his cigarettes. Dad didn't smoke anymore.

I spotted a package of icicles that had got kicked under the occasional chair. "Here's more," I said. "Carrie and I can finish decorating."

"All right," Mom said. "And I'll make some hot cocoa."

We hung the silver icicles, meticulously, from the tip of each branch, and when we were finished the tree was picture-perfect, just like all the years before.

Mom brought the steaming mugs in on a Coca-Cola tray and Dad plugged in the tree lights. There were two strings on the tree but only one lit up.

"Awwww!" we all groaned.

"Just hold your horses," Dad said. Unscrewing the bulbs one by one, he finally found the dud and replaced it with a new one. Then they all glowed at once.

Robbie came in at that moment and whistled his approval. Jimmy, who was already in his PJs, sat cross-legged under the tree, shaking boxes.

Carrie and I looked at all their faces: the coloured tree-lights reflected like rainbows in their eyes. "Are you thinking what I'm thinking?" she whispered to me.

"I think so," I whispered back.

Gathered around the Christmas tree, just the four of us kids with Mom and Dad, it made everything seem normal again. The way it used to be before the second family came along.

Then, right on cue, the wailing of the baby-twins came sailing down the stairs and broke the spell.

"Time for their bottles," Mom said.

"Time for bed," Dad said and he unplugged the tree lights.

* * *

In bed I rotated my feet trying to ease the pain from the too-tight skates out of my ankles.

"Did you have fun tonight?" asked Carrie from the bottom bunk.

"Did I!" I hung over the rail, letting my clean hair stream down like shiny icicles.

"Do you think the boys would have kissed us good-night if Jimmy hadn't been there?" asked Carrie.

"I don't know."

"Well, speculate."

"What does that mean?"

"Take a guess," she said.

"Ummm, well, maybe. When we stopped by the boards for a breather Dale said, 'You have the most interesting eyes.'"

"Hmm," Carrie mused. "That might not be a compliment."

"What else could it be?"

"It might mean strange or eerie."

"Eerie?"

"Yeah. Remember Miss Paddison said the gold specks glittering in our green eyes gave her shivers up her spine? And Robbie always says they make him feel positively eerie."

"Oh, what does he know." I flung my head back up, twisted my hair into a ponytail, fastened it with a rubber band and flopped back onto my pillow. "Who listens to brothers, anyway?"

Carrie laughed. "Let's go to sleep before Santa Claus comes," she said.

We giggled and tried to remember what it was like to be young enough to believe in Santa.

Chapter 17

Christmas Day

Christmas shopping had been lots of fun that year, especially for the babies. We had lumped our money together and bought Jay a big brown teddy bear and Joy a baby doll that wet itself.

Mom had done all her Christmas shopping on the telephone out of the Sears Roebuck catalogue and nothing fit anybody. "Oh, dear, now it will all have to go back," she moaned.

Carrie and I hadn't even tried to outwit each other this year. She bought me the stuff I wanted, and I bought her the stuff she wanted.

Aunt Sylvia and Uncle Phil came to our house for dinner. It was their first childless Christmas.

"We talked for an hour on the phone to Marilyn," Aunt Sylvia said. "And it was wonderful hearing her voice." She sighed wistfully. "She said to thank you for the lovely Christmas box, Sissy."

"I'm glad it got there on time," Mom said. "And maybe next year they'll be home for Christmas.

Meantime you've got us."

We didn't have the traditional turkey dinner because Aunt Sylvia said Uncle Phil was allergic to fowl. Dad said it was all in his head, but he didn't make a fuss about it. I think he felt sorry for them, their only living child being thousands of miles across the sea on Christmas day, and he had all of us. So instead of turkey or goose we had glazed ham garnished with canned pineapple slices and Mom's inimitable (Carrie's new word) scalloped potatoes.

Dessert was not Mom's traditional English plum pudding either. Aunt Sylvia had brought a surprise dessert in a big green box tied with a bright red bow.

"What on earth could it be?" Mom puzzled as she carefully untied the bow and took off the lid. "Oh!" she cried as she lifted out a big round cake the size of a dinner plate. Half of it was frosted blue and the other half pink, and little silver balls spelled out, "Happy Five-Month Birthday to Jay and Joy!" Around the edge of the cake were five pink candles and five blue ones.

Uncle Phil lit the candles and Dad turned out the lights. The flickering flames danced in the babies' eyes like lights on water.

Then we all sang "Happy Birthday," and Jimmy helped the babies blow out their candles.

Afterwards, Dad and Uncle Phil went out for a brisk walk to shake their dinner down. Jimmy rolled around on the carpet holding his stomach and watching television. Robbie went upstairs to practice on his guitar. He was getting good. He had organized a school band and they played at the Friday night high school dances.

Aunt Sylvia was helping Mom wash up at the kitchen

sink. There was nothing for us twins to do, so to Mom's surprise and delight, we offered to put the babies to bed. They chortled and squealed and kicked their fat legs as we struggled to take off their sleepers to change their diapers.

"Oh, no!" gagged Carrie, turning her head away. Sure enough, they'd done their worst.

"Ewww!" I agreed, holding my nose. "I don't think I'll ever be able to eat another hot dog with mustard on it."

"Oh, Connie, how could you!" That was one of our differences. She had a weaker stomach than I had. She just managed to finish changing Jay before she ran, retching, to the bathroom.

We had a good wash and splashed cold water on our faces. The phone was ringing as we went laughing down the stairs.

Mom answered it. "Hello!" she said in her melodic telephone voice. "Yes, Carrie's here. Ye-es, Connie too. Who wants to know?"

We stopped dead at the bottom of the stairs and listened.

"Just a minute." Mom covered the mouthpiece as she held out the phone to Carrie. "It's a boy. Now don't stay on too long. Don't forget, Christmas is a family day. And your dad and uncle will be back any minute."

I knew it was Hunter Davidson by the way Carrie rolled her eyes. "Thanks, Merry Christmas to you, too," she said. She talked for a while, self-consciously, then she handed me the phone. "Somebody wants to speak to you," she said with a glint in her gold-speckled green eyes.

It was Dale Moran. "Hi, Connie," he said. "I just

80

thought I'd wish you a merry Christmas." He had a cute way of pronouncing words, sort of English, like Cary Grant.

"Same to you," I said.

Carrie was right. Christmas had turned out superb that year.

Chapter 18

Duplicity

Lorena Ellsworth and Nancy Case and Carrie and I had been friends ever since first grade. But after our smashing success in the Christmas play things changed.

Carrie said Lorena was positively decimated when she found out that Dale Moran was crazy about me. And Nancy Case refused to believe that Hunter Davidson had a serious crush on Carrie.

"I thought you said your parents wouldn't let you have boyfriends until you're sixteen," Nancy snapped at me.

"Well, they're boys and we're friends," I snapped back.

"Oh, don't be so smart. Anyway, for your information, Hunter Davidson and Lorena Ellsworth are going steady, so your sister shouldn't be trying to steal him. And he even told Lorena that he was in love with her. Has he ever told Carrie that?"

"How should I know?"

"I thought twins knew everything about each other," sneered Nancy.

"Well, you thought wrong," I said. "I have to go now. I promised my mother I'd mind the babies today."

I hadn't promised any such thing but I ran up our walk as if I had. Carrie's coat was already on the hall rack so I knew she was home. I hung mine up and kicked off my galoshes.

"Pssst! Connie!" Carrie was beckoning to me from the top of the stairs. I ran up two at a time. She pulled me into our bedroom and shut the door.

"You won't believe what Lorena Ellsworth told me today," she said.

"You won't believe what Nancy Case just told me," I said. "You go first."

She pushed a pile of stuff off the bottom bunk to make room for us to sit. "Lorena said that Dale Moran was Nancy Case's steady boyfriend and you were trying to steal him off her."

"That's exactly what Nancy Case just told me about you and Hunter Davidson. And she said Hunter told Lorena he was in love with her."

"I don't believe it. Do you believe it?"

"No-o-o. I think they're just jealous."

"CAR-RIE! CON-NIE!" Mom yelled so loud we heard her right through the floor.

"Let's talk later," I said and we hurried down to see what Mom wanted.

"Will you amuse the babies for me?" Mom said. "They haven't given me a moment's peace all day long. I think they're cutting teeth."

"Why can't Jimmy amuse them?" we said.

"Because he's not good with babies. And besides he seems to favour Joy and I don't understand it."

"Well, that's 'cause he's a boy and he's jealous of Jay," I said.

"Really? Which one do you two favour?"

"Neither," Carrie said. "We're sick of them both."

"Well, shame on you for saying such a thing." Mom clucked her tongue. "How would you like it if I said that about you?"

"Oh, she was just kidding, Mom," I said. We each picked up a baby and took them into the living room to play on the carpet.

*　*　*

Robbie had got a brand-new guitar for Christmas. And he had a new job, too. He had auditioned for a band called "The Heartbreaks" and he had been hired as their lead guitarist. They played every weekend at a dance hall called The Blue Moon.

Dad and Mom were skeptical at first. "Is any drinking allowed there?" Mom asked. Mom was death on drinking because her own father had died of the drink, she said.

"No, Mom," Robbie assured her as he lovingly polished his guitar with a soft bit of chamois. "It's a club for teens to keep them off the streets. And parents are volunteer chaperones. You and Dad can be chaperones if you like. Then you'll see for yourself."

"That's good enough for me," Dad said. "Just so long as your grades don't suffer. You need high marks to get into college, you know."

"Don't worry." Robbie was smart and he knew it. He had no trouble keeping up his grades.

Carrie and I had been listening as we dried the dishes. We tried not to let them clatter so we wouldn't miss anything.

"How old do you have to be to go to The Blue Moon?" we asked casually. Ever since Marilyn's wedding we were crazy about dancing and hadn't missed a Friday night junior-high dance.

"It doesn't matter as long as you have your parents' consent," Robbie explained. Then he packed his new guitar carefully into its case and left the kitchen.

"Can we go, Mom?" Carrie took the nerve to ask.

"You're much too young," Mom said.

"We'll be fourteen in May," we protested.

Dad folded his paper and got up from the table abruptly. "It's out of the question," he snapped. Then he went into the living room and shut the French doors, not with a bang, but firmly so that we knew better than to follow him.

"Mom . . . "

"You heard your father."

We pulled long faces as we clattered the dishes into the cupboards. Then we hung up the dish towels and went upstairs.

There was no use arguing, we knew that, so we spread out our books on our oversized desk and turned on our new radio. It was an RCA Victor, no bigger than a bread-box, that our parents had given us for Christmas. Dad had made a shelf for it above our desk.

As it warmed up we heard the soulful voice of Eddie Fisher singing, "Oh! My papa, to me he was so wonderful . . . "

Carrie switched it off.

* * *

On the last Friday in February, a springy day that melted the snow into rivers that ran gurgling down the sewers, we were walking home with Dale and Hunter.

"Hey," Dale said. "How'd you guys like to go dancing tonight?"

"The school dance?" we asked.

"Heck no. I'm sick of school dances. The records are so old and scratchy you can hardly hear them. Besides, there's always teachers there, spying. We're going to The Blue Moon."

"I heard they've got a great band there," Hunter added.

"The Heartbreaks," Carrie said.

"Our brother, Robbie, is the lead guitarist," I bragged.

"No kidding!" Dale sounded impressed.

We stopped at the corner of Jefferson and Newport where we always parted company.

"Wanna go?" Dale asked me.

"Yes but . . . " I hesitated.

"Well, if you decide to, meet us here at seven o'clock. Okay?"

"Okay," Carrie said and we started walking up our street.

"They won't let us go," I said.

"I know," Carrie agreed. "Unless . . . "

"Unless what?" I stopped and looked into her eyes. The gold specks were glittering mischievously.

"Unless Lorena and Nancy go with us."

"They're still mad at us. Remember?"

"Yeah. But Mom and Dad don't know that."

"Uh oh!" I said.

As soon as we walked in the door we hollered down the hall, "Need any help, Mom?"

"Do I! I haven't even had time to fix my hair today." Mom was folding a pile of diapers a mile high on the kitchen table. "You girls finish this job for me while I get the twins up. If they sleep all day they'll be awake all night. Sometimes I think second families are strictly for the birds."

"We've never heard you say that before, Mom."

"Oh, don't listen to me." She was running a comb through her unruly hair at the mirror over the kitchen sink. "I wouldn't be without my baby-twins for all the world."

She didn't need to tell *us* that.

* * *

We had the dishes done and put away by six-thirty. We hadn't even mentioned the dance yet. Robbie had already left for rehearsal and Jimmy was next door playing pool at the Pools' and Dad was on the night shift, so we only had Mom to contend with.

"Mom," we said. She was rocking the twins, with her foot, in the twin rocking-horse Dad had made them for Christmas. "We're going out with Lorena and Nancy tonight. Okay?"

"Where to?" she asked, her foot coming to a standstill.

"To the dance," we said.

"Well, all right, but you four girls stay together. Who's going to drive you there and back?"

We knew Mom thought we were talking about the school dance.

"Mr. Ellsworth," we said. The lies were sliding off our tongues as smooth as ice cream.

"All right. Away you go and have a good time. Thanks

for all your help. I feel much better now."

"You're welcome, Mom," we called over our shoulders as we raced upstairs to get ready. We decided to wear our green taffeta dresses with the huge crinolines underneath and our new patent leather slippers with the little heels. We always got more attention when we were dressed exactly alike. There seemed to be a fascination about identical twins. We were even fascinated with ourselves.

We put on our coats and slipped out the door before Mom could see how we were dressed.

The boys were waiting for us at the corner. Hunter and Carrie walked ahead and Hunter took her hand. So Dale took mine. We walked to The Blue Moon laughing and swinging hands.

* * *

The first person we bumped into there was Robbie, coming out of the boys' washroom. He did a double-take when he saw us. "Does Mom know you're here?" he hissed.

"Sure," we said.

"You'd better not be lying," he said, glaring over his shoulder as he made his way to the stage.

"Are we lying?" I whispered to Carrie as we hung up our coats in the cloakroom.

"Not exactly," she said, puffing out her crinoline. "It's more like duplicity." That sounded pretty good to me. Carrie had the right word for everything.

We heard the band warming up so we hurried out on to the dance floor. Dale and Hunter were standing around waiting for us. Pretty girls in crinolines were everywhere, but we were the only two that looked exactly alike. Dale and Hunter danced with us all night.

The band played "Rock Around The Clock" and "Yellow Rose of Texas" and "Ain't That A Shame" and lots of other songs we'd never heard before. We were having the time of our lives when the band suddenly decided to take a break, just as we were swinging by the stage.

Robbie beckoned us over. "You two better get going," he said in a dead-serious voice. "The dance at your school will be over by now."

He had seen right through our duplicity.

Dale and Hunter walked us back to the corner of Jefferson and Newport. It was dark and cold now. We stood around for a few minutes but they didn't attempt to kiss us. So we said an awkward goodnight and started running up the street. Our ankles kept turning on the heels of our patent leather slippers.

"My feet are killing me." Carrie was almost crying.

As soon as we turned up our walk we saw Mom's face framed in the little square window of the front door.

Flinging it open she demanded, "Where's Mr. Ellsworth?"

"He dropped us off at — "

We didn't get a chance to finish.

"Don't you dare tell me another lie," Mom snapped. "Lorena and Nancy came to call on you tonight."

Our hearts sank.

"Don't tell Dad, please, Mom," we pleaded. "We'll never do it again, we promise!"

"No. I won't tell him," she said.

"Oh, thanks, Mom." We heaved a huge double sigh.

"But you will. In the morning. Now go to bed this minute."

* * *

Dad was sitting at the breakfast table stirring his coffee. "Your mother said you had something to tell me." He spoke without looking at us.

"We're sorry, Daddy," we blurted out. "We'll never do it again."

The word "daddy" usually touched a soft spot in our dad.

He sipped his coffee and didn't say a word.

"We're . . . we're . . . absolutely desolated," Carrie whimpered.

That's when he looked up. "You're absolutely grounded," he growled. "But you're not grounded because you went to that dance." He took off his glasses and glared at us one at a time. "Do you know why you're grounded?"

"Yes, Daddy," we said. "Because we lied about it."

"That's right. I'm glad we understand each other."

* * *

We were grounded for a whole month. By the time we were free again both Hunter and Dale had found new girlfriends. The only consolation was that they weren't Lorena and Nancy. They were two girls from another school. So Lorena and Nancy and Carrie and me made up and became friends again.

Chapter 19

A Knock at the Door

All during the month of March, as part of our punishment, we had not been allowed to watch television, so we studied our heads off instead and we both got straight As. And now that the exams were over we were busy catching up on our favourite programs.

One Saturday night, right in the middle of *Gunsmoke*, a knock came at the front door. Mom looked up, startled. She glanced at the anniversary clock on the mantle: ten o'clock. "Who could that be at this hour?" she said nervously.

Dad wasn't home yet (he had gone to a retirement dinner for Ira Wattles, his friend at the plant) and Robbie was out playing in the band at The Blue Moon.

"I'll get it, Mom," Jimmy said jumping up from the spot he'd worn thin on the Axminster rug.

"Look through the window first," she said.

Jimmy squinted through the sheer curtain that covered the square window. "It's a man in uniform. Shall I let him in?"

"For mercy's sake, no!" cried Mom. "Let me see who it is."

Carrie and I were right on her heels. Nobody ever came to our door unexpectedly on a Saturday night. So we all took turns peering through the curtain.

There was a little snow drift on the visor of the man's cap and his nose was red as a ripe strawberry. Detroit was having a cold snap and it had been snowing since suppertime. Across the pocket of his coat were the words "Western Union."

"*Telegram for Mr. And Mrs. Taylor!*" he shouted through the letter slot.

Mom put the chain on the door and opened it an inch. Cold wind swirled in through the gap. "Slide it through," she said.

"I need a signature, ma'am," the man said, "and I can't get my clipboard through there."

Mom reluctantly opened the door and allowed the man in the Western Union uniform to step inside on the mat. He handed her his clipboard. There was a pencil fastened to it on a dirty string.

He sniffed his nose, drawing up two big drops, and huffed on his hands. Mom signed and he gave her a long yellow envelope.

"I hope it's good news, ma'am," he said. Then he tipped his cap and the snowdrift slid off on the floor. Mom locked the door behind him and put the chain back on. She stood very still, staring at the long envelope in her hand.

"Open it, Mom!" croaked Jimmy. His voice had a tendency to crack when he was excited now.

"Who's it from, Mom?" asked Carrie and I.

"I don't know." Mom turned the envelope over and over in her hands. "I think I'll just keep it until your father comes home."

"Aw, c'mon, Mom. Open it!" we all yelled. We'd never seen a telegram before.

But she walked slowly into the living room and leaned the envelope against the mantle clock. Then she just stood there staring at it.

"What's wrong, Mom?" The strange look on her face gave Carrie and me a funny feeling.

"I don't know," she said. "Maybe nothing . . . but . . . but . . . "

"But what, Mom?" asked Jimmy in his squawky new voice.

"But I've never known a telegram to bring good news," she said. Leaning over, she switched off the television.

"What kind of news does it bring, Mom?" The expression on her face made us whisper the question.

"Does it mean somebody's dead, Mom?" asked Jimmy bluntly.

Carrie gave me a sideways glance.

"Maybe it's Dad or Robbie," suggested Jimmy.

"Weirdo!" we snapped, darting him a shut-your-face glare.

"No, no." Mom shook her head. "A telegram is always from far away."

Far away could mean Toronto, Canada. Or even Nottingham, England, where Mom still had a half-sister that she got a card from at Christmas.

Just then we heard a key turn in the lock.

"Dad! Dad!" We all ran to the door.

"Take the chain off, for Pete's sake!" yelled Robbie through the gap. "A guy could freeze out here."

Jimmy unhooked the chain and Robbie jumped inside and slammed the door.

"What was the chain doing on?" He leaned his guitar case in the corner and rubbed his bright red ears.

"We got a telegram," Jimmy said. "With bad news in it."

"A telegram!" Robbie peeled off his turtleneck and ran his fingers through his wet hair. "Who from? What bad news?"

"We don't know yet," I said.

"Mom won't open it," Carrie said.

"I'll open it when your father gets home," Mom said.

"Where is he?" asked Robbie.

"He's at a retirement party for one of his buddies," Jimmy said.

"That means he won't be home for ages. Let's open it, Mom."

"No." Her mouth was set in a stubborn line. "Not till your father's here."

Another half hour dragged by. We were all so mesmerized by the yellow envelope leaning against the clock that we forgot to turn the Motorola back on.

At eleven o'clock the baby-twins began to howl.

"Will you get them?" Mom said, as if she didn't dare let the telegram out of her sight. "It's time for their night bottle."

Getting the babies up meant changing them, of course. And they both had done their worst, as Dad would say.

We gagged our heads off and Jay and Joy gurgled and

laughed, kicking their fat-creased legs as we struggled with their diapers. It was all we could do not to stick them with the big safety pins.

By the time we carried them downstairs Mom had their bottles warmed up.

"Thank you, girls," Mom said. "I'll have to wean them off this feeding. They don't need it. Look at the size of them!" She held out her arms but the twins clung to us twins like fat leeches, so we sat on the sofa and fed them their bottles.

Just as we were tucking them in at opposite ends of their giant crib we heard the front door open. Then we heard Dad's voice saying, "How come everybody's still up?"

"Dad! Dad!" we screamed, racing down the stairs.

"It's about time you got home," Mom snapped at him.

"What's the panic?" Dad said, slapping his fedora against his knee to knock off the light snow.

"We got a telegraph," Jimmy blurted out.

"Telegram, dopey," corrected Robbie.

"And Mom's afraid to open it," we said.

Mom got the envelope off the mantle and handed it to Dad. He looked at it suspiciously and turned it over in his hands just as she had done.

"Open it, Dad, before we all croak with curiosity," Robbie said.

Dad frowned and shook his head. "Good news never travels by telegram," he murmured, confirming Mom's words in the same mysterious voice.

At last he broke the seal and drew out the telegram. We all held our breath as he read it to himself. Then a big relieved smile spread across his face. "I take it back," he said. "This time good news does travel by telegram."

He cleared his throat and read: "Planning a 25th anniversary party for Lyle and Lily at The Old Mill, Monday, April 2, 1956. Stop. Hope you can make it. Stop. Signed Dave and Rose."

"Can we go, Dad? Can we go?" we squealed, following him into the kitchen. Uncle Dave and Aunt Rose and their two boys, Norman and Bart, were our favourite Canadian relatives.

Dad leafed the kitchen calendar over to April. "That's Easter weekend," he said. "If the weather clears up we should be able to make it."

Chapter 20

Easter in Toronto

We left Detroit early Sunday morning. The air was crisp and clear.

"We'll take the tunnel to save time," Dad said.

"I don't like the tunnel," Mom said, settling the babies in her lap. "It's always dripping with water and I have the feeling it's going to collapse any minute."

"It's built to last," Dad said.

Carrie and I didn't like the tunnel either. It was creepy knowing that the St. Clair River was tumbling over our heads. Dad usually took the scenic route up Highway 94 and over the Blue Water Bridge. That was a nice way to go.

We stopped halfway at a restaurant so Mom could feed the twins their bottles. When we got back in the station wagon Mom handed Carrie and me each a baby. "My arms are nearly paralyzed," she said, stretching them out and flexing her fingers.

Every few minutes she twisted around to check on us. The babies had strands of our long brown hair seized in their fat fists.

"Ow!" we both squealed as they yanked the hair right our of our heads by the roots.

"Do you want me to take them?" Mom asked.

"No, it's okay," we said.

"Jimmy?" Mom said. "Do you want a turn holding one of them?"

Jimmy had the back seat all to himself. Robbie had stayed home alone for the first time in his life. He was minding the house next door for the Pools who had driven down to Florida for the Easter vacation. Betty Pool was mad as hops when her father made her go. She made Robbie promise on a stack of Bibles that he wouldn't even look at another girl while she was away. "She's got hopes," Carrie and I said.

"No thanks," Jimmy answered Mom. "I'm too busy." He was busy reading Archie comic books.

* * *

By the time Flash Gordon pulled into Uncle Dave's driveway in Toronto, four long hours later, Carrie and I were a mess of tangled hair and wrinkled dresses.

The door of the house burst open and Auntie Rose came running out. Flinging open the car door she reached inside for the twins.

"OH!" she cried ecstatically. You'd think she'd never seen babies in her life before. "They're gorgeous. Absolutely, positively, out-of-this-world gorgeous."

Our two boy cousins — well, Norman was nearly a man now — came out the door, followed by Uncle Dave.

"Hi, twins!" Norman said. And he meant us. "Where's Rob?"

"He couldn't come 'cause he's got a job," Jimmy butted in.

Halfway to the car Uncle Dave stopped to light a fresh cigarette from the glowing butt between his fingers. Taking a big drag he instantly went into a coughing fit.

"Dave!" Mom snapped over his barking cough. "You can't smoke around my babies. And if you do we're leaving."

Then Dad did the most unbelievable thing; he snatched the cigarette right out of his brother's mouth and squashed it underfoot on the black asphalt driveway.

"Oww!" Uncle Dave pinched the torn skin off his bottom lip and looked at his fingers. There was blood on them. He dabbed his mouth with his white hanky.

"You heard the boss," Dad said.

Mom rolled her eyes. "You men bring in the suitcases," she ordered as if she really was the boss.

After supper Auntie Rose helped Mom get the babies ready for bed. "Oh," she said, kissing the top of Joy's silky fair head. "You're so lucky to have a second family. It's like being given a second chance."

Mom was holding Jay up over her head, jiggling him gently to make him laugh. Drool spilled from his gurgling mouth onto her cheek and she didn't even mind. "I know," she said. "And I'm going to try to get it right this time."

"And another lucky thing." Auntie Rose beamed at Carrie and me over Joy's head. "You've got two made-to-order babysitters."

Carrie and I just gritted our teeth.

* * *

Uncle Dave had got Bart's crib down from the attic.

"I couldn't borrow another crib for love nor money," Auntie Rose apologized.

"Oh, that's all right," Mom said, tucking a baby at each end. "They're used to sleeping together."

Sure enough they went straight off to sleep. "Out like a light," Dad whispered proudly.

That night we did the most incredibly fun thing. We all sat down around the dining-room table and played poker. Uncle Dave shuffled the deck and Auntie Rose put a cereal bowl in the middle of the table. Everybody had a pile of pennies in front of them and we each had to put a penny in the bowl.

We twins caught on to the game pretty quick because Dad had taught us how to play euchre years ago. But Jimmy caught on even quicker.

"You're one smart little nipper," Uncle Dave said as Jimmy raked in the cash.

"He takes after no stranger," Dad said, puffing out his chest.

"Thank you very much," Mom said, patting her dark wavy hair.

"I think he means his ownself, Mom," explained Jimmy.

"Well, you could have fooled me!" laughed Mom.

That's what we did until way past bedtime — played cards and kidded each other. It was more fun than *I Love Lucy*.

After a late-night snack of Ritz crackers and cream cheese with red pimentos in it, and strawberry jam on buttered toast, we all went to bed.

You had to go downstairs to the bedrooms in their house because it was built upside-down on the side of a hill.

"Well, Davie . . . " we heard Auntie Rose say as she was

closing their bedroom door, "you didn't have a ciggie all night long and you didn't miss them a bit, now did you?"

Uncle Dave coughed on purpose. "Oh, I wouldn't go so far as to say that, Rosie," he said. "It's all a matter of willpower."

Chapter 21

The Old Mill

The next evening the whole Taylor family congregated at The Old Mill. It was an historic building that used to be a real water mill, beside a stream. But now it was a fancy restaurant for dining and dancing.

We all gathered in the lobby waiting to surprise Uncle Lyle and Aunt Lily.

Uncle Dave was stationed at the huge oak door as a lookout.

There was so much babble in the lobby that he couldn't make himself heard, so he put two fingers in his mouth and blew a shrill whistle. "Here they come!" he hollered.

We all gasped and held our breath. You could have heard a pin drop. Then a man in uniform flung open the giant door. "SURPRISE!" we shouted at the top of our collective lungs.

"Oh, no! I can't believe my eyes," cried Aunt Lily, clapping her hand over her mouth. Uncle Lyle just grinned self-consciously. But they were both dressed up in evening clothes and Aunt Lily's bouffant hairdo, stiff as a bird's nest, was topped with a sparkling tiara.

Carrie and I glanced at each other. "Dead giveaway," we said.

After all the kissing and hugging was done a man in a navy-blue uniform with gold braid on his shoulders called out, "Ladies and gentlemen, this way please." Then he led all twenty-five of us into the dining room where a long table had a sign on it which read: RESERVED FOR THE TAYLOR FAMILY.

The wood-panelled dining room had soaring ceilings that glittered with crystal chandeliers. And the long table was decorated with silver wedding bells and silver candlesticks and sparkling silverware. Even the dishes were trimmed in silver.

"Why is everything silver, Mom?" asked Jimmy.

"Because the twenty-fifth is the silver anniversary," she explained.

The guests of honour were seated at either end of the table. The rest of us were lined up along the sides. There were place cards at every setting and you had to sit where you found your own name.

Carrie and I were wedged between our cousins, Peter and Peggy. Peggy was known in the Taylor family as Pretty Peggy because she had won a beautiful-child contest at the Canadian National Exhibition when she was a baby. And her mother never let anybody forget it. Mom and Dad sat across the table beside Auntie Bea and Uncle George.

Everybody wanted to know all about the baby-twins. Auntie Rose had asked her neighbour to babysit so Mom could have a peaceful night out for once.

"I'm dying to see them," exclaimed Auntie Bea. "Who do they look like?"

"Well, Jay's got dark curls like me, and Joy's got her dad's sandy-coloured hair."

"Haven't you got pictures in your purse?" Dad asked Mom.

"I might have one or two," Mom said. Then she pulled out a roll of snapshots three feet long. Everybody ooh-ed and aah-ed as the snapshots were passed up one side and down the other side of the long table. Carrie and I frowned at each other. It used to be us they ooh-ed and aah-ed at.

Jimmy was sitting opposite us between Louise and Anne, Auntie Bea and Uncle George's girls. They had blonde hair and blue eyes and they both wore glasses shaped like seashells. They could have been mistaken for twins, except that Louise was taller and had bigger teeth.

"Do that again," begged Louise, gazing adoringly at Jimmy.

"Please, please!" squealed Anne, her long eyelashes sweeping inside her glasses.

So our show-off little brother went into his act. Bugging his eyes out of his head, he did a perfect imitation of Ricky Ricardo. "No, Lucy," he said in Desi Arnaz's scrapy Cuban-accented voice. "You can't sing with my band. Your voice go through my head like a nail!"

Pretty Peggy laughed and clapped her hands. "Oh, you're so funny, Jimmy!" she cried. "And talented!" Then she turned to me. "Have you got any special talents, Connie?"

"Not unless you count being an identical twin," I said.

"Don't be silly," she scoffed.

Down near the end of the line, Aunt Minnie was examining the pictures. "You've certainly got your hands full with your second family!" she shouted the length of the table at Mom. "Aren't you lucky you've got built-in babysitters?"

"Why does everybody have to say that?" grumbled Carrie.

"I'll bet you're jealous now that you're not the only twins in the family," snickered Peggy.

"Of course they're not jealous," Mom snapped from across the table. "They're big girls now."

Carrie and I exchanged another frown. We didn't know which was worse, to be accused of being jealous of babies, or being called "big girls" when we were almost women.

At last, waiters in maroon uniforms brought us our salads.

"We're having five courses," Aunt Janet announced to everybody. "And I made all the arrangements myself."

"I hate food coming in dribs and drabs," Dad complained. "I like my dinner on my plate all at once."

After the salads came soup. Dad took one spoonful and pulled a funny face. "This soup is cold as winter," he complained.

"Yes, sir, it's supposed to be," explained the waiter.

"For pity's sake, stop complaining." Aunt Janet gave her brother a poke. "We're having French cuisine tonight. The soup is called vichyssoise. You Americans are so gauche!"

Clamping his mouth shut Dad pushed his bowl away and drummed his fingers on the glistening white tablecloth.

The next dish was the entree. It was French, too: chicken stuffed with ham and cheese.

"It's Cordon Bleu," explained Aunt Janet. Then she added teasingly, "Served with French-cut green beans and julienne carrots, and potatoes au gratin."

By this time Dad was starving so he ignored his youngest sister and dug right in.

When the dessert came, it was French too: crème caramel. Then the whole wonderful meal was topped off by a three-tiered wedding cake and delicious, foamy café au lait.

"I'm stuffed to the eyeballs," Dad had to admit, loosening his belt.

Just then we heard music drifting in from the adjoining room. So we all followed the anniversary couple into the glittering ballroom.

A wide banner, stretched above the bandstand, read: JAMES FLANNERY AND HIS DEBONNAIRES. A dapper man in a tuxedo, with slick black hair, tapped the microphone with his fingertip to get everybody's attention. "My first rendition tonight is a special request from the groom," he announced. "'I Married an Angel'!"

Everybody said, "Awww!" and Aunt Lily cried, "Oh, Lyle, you remembered our song."

Aunt Lily didn't look much like an angel to me, except for her tiara, but the way Uncle Lyle gazed at her as he led her out onto the dance floor, I guess he thought she did.

The band played lots of old songs that were popular when they were young: "Did You Ever See a Dream Walking" and "Always" and "Ain't We Got Fun?" And our cousins, Peter and Norman, dutifully asked us to dance.

Between numbers, while we were standing on the sidelines talking to Aunt Minnie and Uncle Emery, two strange boys came over and asked us for a dance. It turned out that the ballroom was open to the public, not just the Taylor family.

"My name's Craig Shuster," said the tall, dark one as he led me onto the dance floor. "What's yours?"

"Connie Taylor," I said.

"You got a funny accent," he said.

"No, I haven't, you have," I said.

Just then Carrie went gliding by in the arms of the other handsome boy. Her head was tilted back and her wavy brown hair was shimmering on her shoulders.

"Your sister's a knockout," Craig said, his eyes following her. Then he looked down at me. "She looks just like you," he added.

"No kidding," I grinned.

Then Carrie and her partner went swinging by again.

This time Craig did a double-take. "You guys must be twins," he said.

"Tell me something I don't know," I quipped.

When the band took a break Carrie and I excused ourselves and went to the powder room. It had gold-trimmed mirrors and gilded water taps.

"It's too bad Robbie isn't here," I said, while we were combing our hair.

"I was thinking the same thing," Carrie said. "He would have loved the Debonnaires. Maybe someday he'll be playing in a place like this."

"I can just picture it." I stretched my arms above my head like an invisible banner. "Rob Taylor and His Heartbreaks."

Pinching our cheeks and biting our lips (Mom wouldn't let us wear makeup yet) we kept talking to each other in the mirror. No wonder Craig did a double-take, I thought. I had to stick out my tongue to make sure I was me.

"What's his name?" Carrie asked as she wet her eyelashes with liquid soap.

"Craig. What's yours?"

"William. I'm sure glad Robbie showed us how to dance."

"Me too. Let's go back out before somebody else nabs them."

But we didn't need to worry, they were right there waiting for us as the band struck up "Bewitched, Bothered and Bewildered."

"There go the belles of the ball," we heard Uncle Emery say as we went two-stepping by. Pretty Peggy gave us a scornful look from the sidelines. We danced with other boys, too, but we ended up having the last dance with Craig and William. Then James Flannery and his Debonnaires signed off with "Some Enchanted Evening."

Mom and Dad had left the party early because of the babies, and Jimmy had gone with them because he was bored. So we went home with Uncle Dave and Auntie Rose.

Both Craig and William had asked for our address. And they promised to look us up if they were ever in Detroit, Michigan.

"Some enchanted evening!" Carrie and I crowed.

Chapter 22

Holiday

The next morning, with our suitcases all packed and ready to go, Auntie Rose suddenly said, "Why don't the girls stay for a couple of days?"

Carrie and I dropped our bags on the hall floor with a simultaneous thud.

"They didn't bring any extra clothes," Mom said.

"They'll be too much trouble," Dad said.

"No, we won't!" Carrie and I protested.

"We'll even do our own washing," I volunteered.

"And I'll take them shopping at Eaton's," Auntie Rose said. "There'll be sales galore right after Easter."

"But how will they get home in time for school?" Mom said.

"Oh, that won't be a problem," said Uncle Dave. "Lyle's got a business appointment in Detroit next week so he'll be able to take them."

So we stayed.

That night Norman and Bart took us to the Runnymede show to see *Love Is a Many Splendored Thing*.

It was a lovely movie, so romantic. And the Runnymede Theatre was fantastic, too. It had a blue domed ceiling with white clouds and shadows of airplanes floating by. After the show Bart and Norman took us to the White Corner restaurant and treated us to hamburgers and Cokes.

* * *

Later, sitting up in Bart's bed that night (Bart said he didn't mind a bit sleeping on the pull-out couch in the recreation room) Carrie and I were writing in our journals. We used to keep diaries when we were young, but now we kept journals.

We were still scribbling an hour later when Auntie Rose poked her head around the door.

"What are you girls writing about?" she asked.

"All about the party at The Old Mill," I said. And Carrie added, "And the movie we saw tonight. It was so romantic." With a roll of her eyes Carrie fell back on the pillow as if she was swooning.

Auntie Rose laughed and dropped a kiss on our foreheads. "I'm glad you're having a good time," she said. "Nighty-night!"

After she shut the door Carrie said, "Want to read what I wrote?"

"Sure," I said, so we exchanged journals.

When we finished reading we handed them back with a grin. Her account was almost identical to mine. Except where I had put Craig's name, Carrie had put William's.

"I wonder how we can let them know we're still in Toronto," Carrie said. That was exactly what I was thinking.

"I'll bet Bart will know how," I said.

"Let's ask him tomorrow," she said.

Then we snapped the lights off on either side of the bed and slid down under the covers.

"Ginny-winny-ninny-gite," we said to each other.

* * *

When we got up the next morning Bart had already gone out and Norman and Uncle Dave had gone to work. The upside-down house was so quiet with no babies squalling that we had slept in till nine o'clock. We had breakfast alone: pancakes smothered in French Canadian maple syrup.

Auntie Rose had the *Toronto Star* spread out in front of her at the other end of the table.

"This looks like a good day to go shopping," she said, pointing to the ad in the paper. "Eaton's has girls' dresses on for half price."

"We didn't bring any extra money," we said.

"Your uncle left some on the counter," she said.

There were two purple ten-dollar bills and one blue five-dollar bill. We loved Canadian money because it was so pretty compared to ours. Ours was all the same shade of green so a one-dollar bill looked exactly like a hundred. Not that we'd ever seen a hundred but we were pretty sure it was the same.

We walked to Bloor Street and got on a red streetcar. Auntie Rose paid our fare and we hurried down the car to the circular seat at the back. Then we had to transfer to a southbound car at Yonge Street. The streetcars joggled jerkily along the tracks and by the time we got downtown we were both feeling queasy.

"Oh, dear," Auntie Rose said. "You look a bit green around the gills. But you'll be all right as soon as we get off."

Sure enough, after a couple of deep breaths of fresh air wafting up Yonge Street from Lake Ontario, we felt better.

Eaton's was a beautiful, big department store, every bit as nice as Crowley's in Detroit. We went up on the elevator to the fourth floor and Auntie Rose let us pick our own dresses from the half-price rack.

We decided to get the same dresses, white with blue polka-dots and a wide patent leather belt, because we were enjoying all the attention we were getting in Toronto. Everywhere we went people said to Auntie Rose, "Identical twin daughters, aren't you lucky! How do you tell them apart?"

Auntie Rose laughed and responded, "Oh, that's a family secret." Then she winked at us and whispered, "What they don't know won't hurt us."

The streetcars were packed on the way back, with Torontonians coming home from work. We had to stand all the way. I thought I'd throw up, hanging on to the bar above my head and being pushed and jostled. At last we got off at Windermere Avenue and followed Auntie Rose into Ligget's Drugstore. Auntie Rose had to buy Aspirin because she had a headache. We said we hoped we didn't give it to her.

"Don't be silly. Of course not," she assured us. "I always get a headache when I go downtown. I call it my exhilaration headache."

I could see Carrie storing up that word in her head.

While Auntie Rose was looking around to see if she needed anything else, Carrie and I browsed through a rack of postcards with scenes of Toronto on them. We each picked out two. We both got Casa Loma, a real castle which we hadn't seen yet — Norman had promised to take us there. I bought "Sunset over Centre Island" and Carrie bought a Canadian National Exhibition postcard with a picture of the Queen on it.

* * *

After supper we finally got a chance to speak to Bart alone, when the three of us went for a walk around the block. There was something we were dying to ask him.

"How can we get in touch with those two boys we were dancing with at The Old Mill?" we asked.

"Do you know their names?"

"Craig Shuster," I said.

"William Smith," Carrie said.

"No use looking for Smith in the phone book," Bart said. "There's thousands of Smiths in Toronto. But we might find a Shuster."

Back at the house Bart looked up Shuster in the telephone directory. There was a whole column of Shusters and he called every one, but nobody knew a Craig Shuster. With a sigh of disappointment we decided to give up.

Norman was home that night because his girlfriend was sick with the flu. So he and Bart played euchre with us until we all got tired of it.

"Come in and watch the news with us," invited Auntie Rose.

Their television was a fourteen-inch Admiral, the kind Dad said he wouldn't give houseroom to. We were surprised to see President Dwight Eisenhower and his wife, Mamie, strolling across the White House lawn with some important-looking people.

"I like Ike," Uncle Dave said.

"Our dad does, too," we said.

The rest of the news was boring so we excused ourselves and went to bed. We wrote our postcards to Mom and Aunt Sylvia and Lorena and Nancy and stuck a Queen stamp on each one. Then we exchanged them to compare what we wrote. As usual, they were almost identical.

* * *

On our last full day in Toronto, Bart took us to a Saturday matinee at the Esquire; that was the other theatre that was within walking distance of their house.

There was a long lineup when we got there, so we had to wait. One of Bart's friends came up behind us in line and they started talking. Carrie and I just stood there, shifting our feet, then she suddenly grabbed my arm. "Look up there at the front of the line," she said. "Isn't that — "

"Yes, it is!" I cried. "It's Craig and William."

Just as we spotted them, they spotted us. Craig waved and came back to the end of the line.

"Hi!" he said.

"Hi!" we said.

"Do you want to come to the front of the line with Will and me? You'll end up sitting in the front row if you stay back here."

"We'd love to," Carrie and I said, "but we're with our cousin Bart."

Hearing his name, Bart turned around. He took in the situation at a glance. "You go ahead," he said. "I'll meet you out front after the show."

So we joined Craig and William and they even paid our admission. We sat in the middle of the back row and held hands through the whole movie. My hand got a cramp in it but I didn't care.

Bart was waiting for us out the front. Then we all went to Rich's Dairy Bar on Bloor Street and shared two bricks of Neapolitan ice cream. The waitress cut them up and served them on little plates and gave us each a spoon. And Craig and William paid for both bricks.

That night at the supper table, Uncle Dave asked, "What movie did you kids see?"

Carrie and I darted each other a quick glance. Then we looked hopefully at Bart.

"The Texas Ranger," he said. "It was swell, wasn't it, twins?"

"Swell," we said. "Really swell."

* * *

The next day, Sunday, we spent the afternoon packing. That night Craig and William came over to say goodbye. Auntie Rose didn't invite them in, so we put on our coats and went out on the front porch. The porch was small, not like our big veranda, so there was no place to sit down. Craig and William had to stand back to back. I was facing Craig and Carrie was facing William so we couldn't see each other.

"How about a little kiss?" I heard William whisper to Carrie.

"How about it?" she answered coyly.

Then Craig said, "Can I . . . may I . . . " All of a sudden he turned apple red. "Can I kiss you goodbye?" he whispered hoarsely.

"Okay," I whispered back.

Our lips had no sooner touched than the door flew open. We jumped apart as if we'd been stung by a bee.

Cough! cough! barked Uncle Dave. He had a cigarette in one hand and his Ronson lighter in the other. (Auntie Rose made him smoke outside in hopes it would discourage the "filthy habit").

"You girls go inside and finish packing," Uncle Dave ordered in a cranky voice we hadn't heard before. "Your Uncle Lyle will be here first thing in the morning." Then he snapped at the boys, "Off you go!" and he dismissed them with a wave of his hand.

"Darn," Carrie and I fumed.

* * *

Uncle Lyle drove all the way to Detroit, Michigan without stopping. (Well, almost without stopping — we had to show our birth certificates at the border and Uncle Lyle had to show his driver's licence.) He was on a business trip and he couldn't afford to waste time, he said. It was a terrible trip.

Chapter 23

Home Again

The baby-twins recognized us the instant we walked in the door. They gurgled and laughed and held up their fat little arms. We swooped them up and kissed and hugged them and let them pull our hair. We didn't realize how much we'd missed them. And we could hardly believe how much they'd changed in a week.

Mom said they were growing like string beans. Joy could almost walk if you let her hold your fingers, and Jay was pulling himself up on all the furniture.

Another thing we couldn't help but notice was how messy our house looked after being at Auntie Rose's where everything was neat and tidy. There were baby toys everywhere and piles of diapers and baby clothes all over the dining-room table. Also, a gate had been stretched across the top and bottom of the stairs to keep the babies safe. What a nuisance it was, having to unlock and lock the gates every time you had to go upstairs to the bathroom.

And everything had to be moved out of reach

because the babies weren't contented in their playpen anymore: knick-knacks and picture frames and ashtrays and ornaments and Mom's vase of artificial flowers. It made the messy house seem oddly empty.

That night, for our welcome-home supper, Mom had made our favourite dessert, lemon meringue pie. We were all enjoying it around the kitchen table and Carrie and I were both talking at once, telling them all about our visit to Toronto, when we heard a strange strangling noise.

"The babies!" Mom screamed. Both she and Dad leapt out of their chairs and raced to the living room. There was Jay, gagging and choking and turning red as a beet. Dad grabbed him up, flung him upside down and thumped him on the back. Out spewed a mess of jujubes all over the Axminster rug. And there sat Joy gleefully banging the empty jujube can on the coffee table.

Nobody would own up to having left the can of jujubes within reach of the babies.

* * *

"I don't know what we're going to do," Mom said that night. She had put the twins to bed and collapsed like a rag doll into her armchair. "Those two babies can't be left alone for five seconds. And they can't share the same bed much longer either. They're already fighting for territory. They need their own space, and two cribs won't fit into our bedroom."

Dad lowered his newspaper and took off his reading glasses. Tapping the frame on his lower lip he said, "We might have to move."

"MOVE!" Carrie and I exploded. "From our *house?*"

"We're going to need more bedrooms eventually,"

Dad said. "Even if we don't have any more kids."

"MORE KIDS!" This time it was Mom who exploded. "Don't even think about it."

Robbie glanced up from his homework spread out on the dining-room table. "You better be kidding, Dad," he said.

"Maybe next time we'll get triplets," Jimmy said. "The Cramptons have nine kids, so why can't we?"

He was serious!

Mom's eyes nearly rolled out of her head. "If I hear another word about more kids I'll scream," she threatened.

"There's a new subdivision going up near the Ford plant." Dad adroitly changed the subject. "It's close enough I could walk to work."

"We couldn't afford a new house, could we?" Mom's eyes narrowed thoughtfully.

"We'd have to take on a bigger mortgage," Dad said. "And that would mean tightening our belts a notch or two."

"If I tighten my belt any more," Jimmy said, patting his flat stomach, "I'd cut myself right in half."

"I could get a job," Robbie said, shutting his books. "I don't need to go to college." He was in his last year of high school.

"You're going!" cried Mom and Dad.

All of a sudden Jimmy jumped up and turned off the Motorola. "Well, I'm not moving!" he declared.

"Why not, Sport?" Dad sounded as if he'd already made up his mind.

"Because I'm not leaving my girlfriend." Jimmy was standing with his feet apart and his arms folded and his bottom lip was jutting out like a shelf.

"Girlfriend!" We all roared laughing.

"It's not funny!" Jimmy cried, the shelf beginning to quiver.

"Mary Ann Polanski asked me would I be her boyfriend and I said yes."

Mom rolled her eyes to the ceiling. "At eleven years old, you are far too young to even think about girls," she said.

"I am not," pouted Jimmy.

"Yes, you are, Sport," Robbie said. "You have to pay their way to movies and buy them popcorn and sodas and chocolates on Valentine's Day. That's why I'm broke all the time."

Suddenly, Dad popped up out of his La-Z-Boy and snapped the television back on. "Everybody shut up or go to bed," he barked.

When the tube warmed up Dad's favourite program, *Father Knows Best*, had already begun.

"Look at that silly Jane Wyatt, all dressed up like a doll," Mom said sarcastically as the mother on the show flitted around her immaculate kitchen in her frilly apron like a butterfly. "What mother could look like that in the middle of making dinner," she huffed.

"Jane Wyatt's a fine-looking woman," Dad said teasingly. "And she always listens to her husband 'cause father knows best."

"Huh!" Mom huffed again. "That's a fairy tale if I ever heard one."

Dad could hardly keep the grin off his face.

Chapter 24

Aunt Sylvia's

We stopped in at Aunt Sylvia's house on the way home from school the following Monday. She was always home on Mondays because her shop was closed.

"Well, look who's here!" she cried, clapping her hands.

She had changed while we were away too. She had bleached her hair platinum blonde and she was sporting black false eyelashes and gold hoop earrings, and she was wearing a red silk caftan. Mom said Aunt Sylvia had always been stylish — after all, she was in the beauty business — but since Marilyn had left she had been depressed and let herself go a bit. But now that spring was here she seemed to have emerged, like a butterfly out of her cocoon.

Getting us each a Coke out of the fridge, she sat down, crossed her legs, and balanced her sling-back slipper on her big toe.

"So . . . what's new?" she said. "Did you have fun in Toronto?"

"Yes, but . . . "

"But what?"

"We might have to move," Carrie said.

"Because of the baby-twins," I added.

"Yes, I know," she said. "Your mother told me. But you can't blame the babies."

"Yes we can, because they've split our family in two. Mom calls us big kids her first family and the baby-twins her second family."

"That's just in a manner of speaking," Aunt Sylvia said.

"No it isn't. Everybody says that. Mrs. Mortimer down the street and our Aunt Minnie in Toronto . . . "

"Well . . . you know what I always say."

"What?"

"It's the things you worry about the most that hardly ever happen."

Aunt Sylvia was usually right, so we went home feeling much better.

But the feeling went away the second Dad stepped in the door.

"I think I've found it," he announced, tossing his hat on the hall tree.

"Found what?" Jimmy was sprawled on the floor reading Tarzan comics.

"Our new house," Dad said.

Carrie and I gasped and Jimmy banged his head on the floor.

"Explain," Mom said, wiping her hands on her apron. "You know I hate surprises."

"Well, Bill Walker — he's my new helper down at the plant — we went to have a look at the new subdivision on our lunch hour. And I think I've found the very house for us." He put his hands on his hips. "And guess what the sign says?"

"What?" Jimmy took the bait.

"It says: 'The perfect second-family house. If you have teenagers and little ones, this is the house for you.'"

"What does that mean, exactly?" asked Carrie and I.

"It means the house has five bedrooms," Dad explained. "And a lot more that this house doesn't have."

"Did you buy it?" asked Jimmy.

"It's just a model, Sport," Dad said. "The actual houses won't go up until fall."

Carrie and I breathed a sigh of relief. The spring buds were just popping open on the trees on Newport Street, so fall seemed ages away.

That night in bed, Carrie said, "I hope we don't have to move."

"Me too," I agreed. "I like our house and I like our school and I like living near Aunt Sylvia. Heck, I even like Mrs. Mortimer."

"Me, too," Carrie laughed. "So let's not complain about anything anymore. Especially about the twins."

"Right," I said. "Especially about the twins."

Chapter 25

Fourteen

"It's the first day of May already," Mom said, tearing April off the kitchen calendar. "I wonder what's so special about May?"

We looked up from our Rice Krispies to see if she was kidding. The twinkle in her big blue eyes told us that she was. "Your birthday's only two weeks away," she said. "How do you want to celebrate it this year?"

"Well, how about you, Mom? It's your birthday, too," we said.

"I'll be forty-four," she said with a sigh. "That's not much to celebrate. But you'll be fourteen. Now that's special."

We looked at the clock and realized if we didn't hurry up we'd be late for school. "We'll think about it and let you know, okay, Mom?"

"Okay," she said as she kissed us goodbye.

But we didn't have time to even think about our birthdays because we were too involved in our studies. We were both working our heads off on important science projects which our teachers had told us would account for fifty percent of our final marks. And we were both determined to get into high school with straight As.

So our birthday didn't even enter our heads again for a week and a half, when Mom brought the subject up at the supper table on Friday night. "Would you like a little party?" she asked. "I think I could manage that if you don't invite too many."

Carrie and I looked at each other. Then we looked around the kitchen. The house was clean, of course, as our Mom was very particular, but there was baby paraphernalia everywhere. It was the same upstairs and down. We didn't know what to say because we didn't want Mom to know what we were thinking. Then Robbie came unexpectedly to our rescue.

"I got an idea," he said, while slathering butter on a roll.

"What?"

"How about The Blue Moon? We got a great guest singer tomorrow night. That's close enough to your birthday."

"Gee, that's sounds swell," Carrie said. "But who would we dance with? We haven't got dates for tomorrow night."

"Oh, lots of guys and girls come by themselves. You two won't have to worry; you'll be danced off your feet."

We glanced at each other and I knew what Carrie was thinking: that sounds like a compliment!

Then I said, "But what about Mom? It's her birthday too."

"Mom and Dad can come too," Robbie said. "We just happen to need chaperones tomorrow night."

Mom looked delighted at the idea. "I've always wanted to hear your band, Robbie," she said. Then she looked at Dad, who hadn't said a word yet. "What do you say, dear?" We hadn't heard her call him that in a month of Sundays.

Dad was cutting up his minute steak. He always cut up his meat all at once even though Mom told him it was good manners to cut it up a piece at a time.

When it was all cut up in bite-sized pieces he put his knife and fork down. "Sounds fine to me," he said. "We'll go to dinner first, then we'll go trip the light fantastic."

Then, to our amazement he jumped up and did a little jig. Sitting back down, his cheeks turning pink (I think he was blushing a bit), he laughed. "Your mother and I used to go dancing every Saturday night before all you kids came along. I think we might still remember how."

Mom's cheeks had turned pink, too. With memories, I thought. "I wonder what I should wear?" she said.

Robbie laughed. "It's not The Old Mill, Mom. You don't have to dress up."

* * *

The next day, Saturday afternoon, we all went to The House Of Beauty and Aunt Sylvia did our hair herself. And when Mom tried to pay her, Aunt Sylvia said, "Your money's no good around here, Sis. And I'll mind the twins, too. How's that for a birthday present?"

We all thanked her profusely, then went home to start getting ready.

Carrie and I decided on the polka-dot dresses we'd bought in Toronto. With the wide patent leather belts cinching in our waists and the crinolines puffing out our skirts we looked like a couple of ballerinas.

Mom wore her second best dress, a blue crepe de chine that made her eyes shine like sapphires. Dad wore his Sunday suit and best shirt and tie.

We went to dinner at Chicken Joy and Dad had a glass of root beer and Mom and Carrie and I each had a pink Shirley Temple with a maraschino cherry in it. It was delicious.

We got to The Blue Moon just as the band was warming up on stage. Robbie saw us from behind the drums and waved a drumstick at us.

"I hope he plays the guitar as well," Dad said. "That thing cost me a fortune."

It was seven-thirty and the place was filling up with teenagers. Some of the kids knew our parents and came over to say hello.

Mom looked around the dance hall and smiled approvingly. The ceiling was painted a cloudy white and big blue moons with painted faces hung down on wires. That's how the place got its name.

The first piece the band played was, "Three Coins in the Fountain" and we no sooner had our coats off than two boys came up and asked us to dance.

Next they played, "Hey There (You With the Stars in Your Eyes)" and we kept on dancing with the same boys. Then they played "Secret Love" (we had the record at home, sung by Doris Day) and two new boys cut in.

Mom and Dad stayed on the sidelines, sitting on a comfortable couch especially provided for the chaperones. They were both smiling and tapping their feet to the music.

We never stopped dancing until the band took their

break. Then we went to the washroom, freshened up, and came back just in time to hear Robbie introducing the soloist, Charlie Sullivan. He was a slim young man with reddish hair, a big nose, and a shabby suit that showed his ankles. But when he opened his mouth out came the voice of an angel and you completely forgot what he looked like. He sang "Mister Sandman" and "Blueberry Hill" and "Melody of Love," one after the other.

During the thunderous applause we saw Robbie talking into Charlie's ear. Then, when the applause died down, Robbie took hold of the mike.

"Charlie has agreed to do me a favour and sing 'Always' especially for my mom and dad who are here with us tonight. I think I've heard them say it's their favourite."

Wild applause as we dragged our reluctant parents onto the dance floor.

Then, with a voice as velvety as Nat King Cole's, Charlie sang "I'll be loving you always, with a love that's true, always . . . "

All we young people stood in a big circle and watched as my parents danced with the ease of Fred Astaire and Ginger Rogers.

We'd never seen them in that light before: Dad, suave in his best grey suit, his fine brown hair combed back in waves, looking down into Mom's blue eyes. Mom, radiant in blue crepe de chine, her cloud of black wavy hair framing her pretty face. No-one would ever guess that they had six kids and the cares of the world on their shoulders.

"Connie," Carrie whispered to me, "aren't they beautiful!" I couldn't answer for the lump in my throat.

All the songs the band played after that were nice and smooth. I think Robbie must have chosen them.

Then Robbie announced that it was our birthdays . . . his mother's and his twin sisters' . . . and the night ended with the whole gang of kids singing us "Happy Birthday"!

Chapter 26

The Switcheroo

We hadn't been in a speck of trouble all year long, ever since we'd been put in separate homerooms. Then — maybe it had something to do with being fourteen — the week before the summer vacation, Carrie got herself in trouble.

"Darn," Carrie said. She was looking in the mirror, carefully arranging her shiny brown bangs across her forehead. "I've got swimming today and I don't want to get my hair wet." Aunt Sylvia had styled her hair the night before while I was studying math at Nancy Case's house. Nancy was extra good in math. "Will you switch with me, Connie?"

"Sure," I said. So we switched clothes and I gave her my math homework and she gave me her gym bag with her swimsuit and cap in it.

Before swim class began I jumped in the deep end of the pool and started treading water in circles. The swimming instructor, Miss Sinclair, a big woman with a perpetual tan and hairy armpits, came to the edge of the pool with her hands on her wide hips. "Caroline Taylor!" she hollered. "Get out of there this minute."

I climbed out, not knowing why, because other kids were treading around the deep end.

"What did I do?" I demanded.

"Sit on that bench and wait," she ordered.

My teeth chattering (Carrie had forgotten to put a towel in her bag) I sat down on the wet wooden bench while the swimming instruction went on without me. When it was over Miss Sinclair came and glared down at me over her folded, muscly arms. Glancing at her man-sized waterproof watch, she snapped, "I'll deal with you tomorrow, Miss." Then, with a squish of her big rubber shoes, she turned on her heel and left me sitting there shivering from head to toe and wondering what I'd done wrong.

Carrie joined me in the cafeteria at lunch time. "I think you're in trouble with Miss Sinclair," I said.

"Oh, no, not with her! What did you do?" she asked. So I told her.

"Darn," Carrie said. "I forgot to tell you that I didn't pass my deep water test yet. I'm not allowed in the deep end."

"Well, then you can't blame me," I shrugged. "You should have told me. And I nearly froze because you forgot your towel. Anyway, Miss Sinclair said she'd deal with you tomorrow."

The next day Carrie got an hour detention so I walked home with Nancy and Lorena.

Nancy and I were best friends again because Barbara Hastings had moved to Royal Oak when her dad had changed jobs.

"We're going to the show Saturday night," Nancy said. "Do you and Carrie want to come?"

"We promised Mom we'd watch the babies Saturday night," I said.

"It must be awful having to mind babies all the time," Lorena said with an unmistakable smirk. She was so proud of her only-child status.

"We don't have to mind them," I said. "Only if we want to."

"I heard my father say he feels sorry for your father," Nancy said, giving Lorena a knowing look.

"Why?" I asked.

"Well, I heard him telling my mother that having a second family is a terrible burden on a man. It's like the straw that broke the camel's back, my dad said."

I felt the hair on the back of my neck bristle up. "Well, my dad doesn't mind a bit," I retorted. "In fact, he's talking about buying a bigger house with ten rooms just in case we have more kids."

Lorena and Nancy shrieked laughing. Then we went into Cunningham's Drug Store for an ice cream soda and, thankfully, the subject changed to boys.

But I wished I hadn't told them any of our business. Dad said the neighbours were nosy in our neck of the woods and he didn't like neighbourhood gossip. Especially about our family.

Chapter 27

A Sunday Drive

"We did it! We did it!" Carrie and I screamed, waving our report cards. It was the end of June and both of us had achieved our goal: we were on our way to high school with straight As. The boys had passed with good grades, too, so Dad surprised us by taking us all downtown to see the musical *Oklahoma* at the new Odeon Theater. We sang "The Surrey with the Fringe on Top" all the way home.

Then the next day, after church, Dad sprang another surprise. Scraping his chair back from the table after lunch, he asked, "Who'd like to go for a nice Sunday drive now that it's stopped raining?" It had rained steadily for a week but now the sun was shining and the ancient trees overhanging Newport Street formed a tunnel of sparkling green leaves.

"What about the babies?" Mom had just put them down for their afternoon nap. "By the time they wake up it'll be time to start supper."

"Give Sylvia a ring," Dad said. "If she can watch them

then we'll make a day of it and have supper at The Toddle Inn."

Mom hesitated, but I could see she was tempted. Since the baby-twins had been born Mom said she was virtually housebound.

Aunt Sylvia came right over.

"I've got their suppers all ready, Sissy," Mom said, showing her the pink and blue covered bowls in the fridge, filled with Gerber's baby food. "You put hot water in the bottom and wait until the food comes to room temperature and . . . "

Aunt Sylvia gave a perfect imitation of Mom rolling her eyes. "I know how it's done, Sis," she said.

"I know you do," Mom apologized. "So we'll leave you now and see you later."

* * *

We drove along the waterfront in Flash Gordon with Dad whistling, "Home on the Range" in that high-pitched whistle of his.

As we sped past the Ford plant Dad said, "That's where I spend most of my time."

"Can we go in and see your assembly line?" asked Jimmy.

"It's not operating on Sundays," Dad said. "But I'll take you there one of these fine days so you can see where your bread and butter comes from."

"Do they make bread and butter in there as well as cars?" Jimmy asked.

We all laughed and Jimmy hung his head in embarrassment. Sometimes he said the dumbest things. Then other times he'd astound us by saying something incredibly clever. Carrie said Jimmy was an enigma.

After nearly an hour's drive — we were outside of the city now, practically in the country — Dad pulled off the paved highway onto a muddy sideroad. Gradually the sideroad got narrower and ruttier and came to a sudden dead end.

"We'll have to walk from here," Dad said.

A huge wooden sign shaped like an arrow read: WELCOME TO WOODLANDS!

Mom gazed around at the empty landscape. "There's not a tree in sight," she said.

"There will be," Dad assured her.

Loose planks had been laid end to end, forming a walkway, and people were picking their way along them, trying not to step off into the mud.

At the end of the walkway, in a sea of mud, stood five new houses.

Dad led us to the house with the "Two Family" sign on it.

Lots of people were milling around the smaller houses; but nobody seemed interested in the big two-family house. It was a large square red-brick house with a little cement porch, hardly big enough to sit on. The porch had a wrought iron railing around it.

"Can we go in?" asked Jimmy.

"We'd track mud," Mom said.

"Take off your shoes and leave them on the porch," Dad said.

We followed him up the three cement steps and kicked off our muddy shoes. The porch was so small that our shoes practically covered it.

"Where would we put our glider?" Carrie and I frowned.

"Oh, my!" Mom said as her stocking feet sunk into the wall-to-wall carpet in the entranceway.

Just as we were crowding in behind her, a salesman popped out of the living room.

"Come in, come in." He beamed at Mom and Dad. "Take your time. Have a good look around."

Mom stepped through the wide archway into the living room. "I prefer French doors," she whispered to Dad, glancing over her shoulder at the beaming salesman.

The huge living room was full of new-smelling furniture covered in clear plastic. Real logs were piled up in a fieldstone fireplace. At the end of the living room another archway opened into a big dining room where a long table was set for dinner.

A narrower archway led into the kitchen.

Mom passed a critical eye over the gleaming white kitchen cupboards, the black-and-white checkered floor and the matching gold-coloured fridge and stove.

"How do you like it?" Dad asked her.

"It's . . . nice," Mom said. "But it's a bit small."

The biggest room in our house on Newport Street was the kitchen. Mom called it her farm kitchen. We almost always ate there, except when we had company.

"There's a breakfast nook, too." Dad pointed to a little alcove in the corner with built-in table and benches.

"It wouldn't hold all of us," Mom said.

"I'm bored," groaned Jimmy.

"Let's have a look upstairs," Dad suggested. We followed him up the hardwood staircase.

On the second floor were five big bedrooms, all beautifully furnished. The master bedroom even had a bathroom of its own.

"It's called *ensuite*," Dad told Mom proudly.

"Where would our bedroom be, Dad?" we asked.

"Take your pick," he said, pointing down the long hall. "You'd each have your own room."

We just gaped at each other. We had never in our life expected to have rooms of our own. The rooms we chose were side by side. Each was furnished with a canopy bed, dressing tables, and closets with full-length mirrors.

"We won't be able to talk to each other," I said.

"We could make up a tapping code and talk through the wall," Carrie said.

Opposite our rooms was the babies' room (you could tell by the furniture) and beside it, the family bathroom. It was twice as big as ours at home, and everything in it was turquoise blue, even the toilet bowl.

"Connie! Carrie!" Jimmy was waving from the doorway at the end of the hall. "Come and see my room! There's a car in here!"

We thought he must be hallucinating, but sure enough there was a car in his room; at least, a bed shaped like a car: a Ford convertible!

Mom and Dad had come down the hall to see what Jimmy was shouting about. Then, all of a sudden Jimmy frowned. "Hey . . . " he said. "What about Robbie?"

"I'm glad you asked," Dad said. "Follow me."

So we all trooped after him down two flights of stairs to the basement. But it wasn't a cement basement like ours on Newport Street, it was a panelled recreation room with a carpeted floor and another bedroom and bathroom!

"He'll be able to bang his drums to his heart's content down here without driving us all crazy," Dad said.

"Well, what do you think?" Dad asked Mom when we had seen the whole house and were back outside putting on our muddy shoes.

"It's . . . nice," Mom said looking around. "But it's a long way from downtown. And why on earth would they call it Woodlands when there's not a tree in sight?"

"They're planning a bus route downtown," Dad said. "And mature trees will be planted in front of every house."

"How near are the schools?" Mom asked.

"They're building a new one right down the street," Dad said. "It's supposed to be ready by fall."

"Is there a high school near here?" Carrie and I asked.

"No, you two will have to take a bus," Dad said.

"Can we keep the new furniture?" asked Jimmy. We could tell by the glint in his eyes that he was thinking of the Ford convertible.

"No," Dad said. "The furniture doesn't come with the house."

On the way home Dad kept his promise and took us to The Toddle Inn restaurant for dinner.

"You can order anything you like," he told us.

"Magnanimous!" whispered Carrie and I.

It must be mental telepathy, I thought. I actually picked up that big word before she said it.

* * *

That night, in our bunk beds, we couldn't seem to settle down.

"Did you like the new house?" Carrie asked.

I sat up suddenly and bumped my head on the

ceiling. "Ow!" I rubbed my head. "I think I've outgrown this bed."

"Me too," agreed Carrie. "Mine sags in the middle."

Hanging over the top rail, I let my hair stream down like a waterfall.

"Well, did you?" she asked.

"Did I what?"

"Like the new house."

"Sort of," I said. "I like the idea of my own space."

"Me, too," Carrie agreed. "But . . . would you want to live in Woodlands?"

"Not really," I said.

"Me neither," she said. "There isn't even a veranda. Where would our glider go?"

"And there's no trees. How long does it take for trees to grow as big as the ones on Newport Street?"

"About a hundred years," she said.

"Our old furniture would look awful in that big house," I said.

"But how could Dad afford all the new stuff we'd need?" Carrie asked.

"I guess he'd have to take two mortgages," I said. But I didn't really know what I was talking about because I didn't understand a thing about mortgages.

That night we both dreamed about the new house and the next morning we told each other our dreams. In our dreams we had both rebuilt the new house, giving it a big kitchen, a wide veranda and French doors between all the rooms instead of archways.

Robbie was eating a big bowl of Wheaties when we came down for breakfast. "Well, did you guys like the new house?" he asked. He hadn't come with us because he'd had to practice two new Elvis Presley songs on his guitar.

"It's okay," we said.

Jimmy said, "I like this house better," in spite of the bed shaped like a Ford convertible.

"So, I didn't really miss anything," Robbie shrugged.

"Except dinner at The Toddle Inn," we said. "Dad let us order whatever we liked."

"Big deal." Robbie got up from the table and put his bowl in the sink. "I had dinner at the Pools'. Barbecued T-bones."

"Then you didn't miss a thing," we said.

Chapter 28

Wonderful News

The next night Mom seemed particularly happy in her farm kitchen.

"I finally found time to make a scrumptious dessert," she said. Then she set her famous orange cake on the table and handed Dad the bread knife to slice it with.

Dad heated the knife in the steam from the kettle. The hot blade sank into the layer cake as smooth as butter, releasing a tantalizing orangey aroma that filled my mouth with water.

Mom scooped up a bit of icing flecked with orange rind and licked her finger. "Mmm," she said, smacking her lips. "Dee-licious, if I do say so myself."

We each got a thick, moist wedge, lying on its side on paper plates to save dishes.

One wedge was left over on the cake plate and Jimmy was eyeing it like a hawk.

Just then Aunt Sylvia breezed in the kitchen door.

"I've got news," she cried breathlessly.

"What news, Sissy?" asked Mom expectantly.

"My Marilyn is coming home!" announced Aunt Sylvia.

Marilyn and Darrell had been in Germany for eight months now.

"Is Darrell being posted home already?" Mom asked.

"No. Marilyn's coming home alone," Aunt Sylvia said.

Dad got a chair from the dining room and set it at the corner of the table for Aunt Sylvia to sit on. Mom served her the last wedge of cake. Jimmy groaned because he'd gobbled his piece up, expecting to get more. Mom laughed and shoved the cake plate, still littered with moist crumbs and bits of orange icing, across the oilcloth towards him.

Then she poured Aunt Sylvia a cup of tea and sat down beside her. "Why is she coming home alone?" she asked.

"Don't tell me there's trouble in paradise," quipped Robbie.

"What's that mean?" asked Jimmy.

"It means the honeymoon is over," Robbie quipped again.

"Is it, Aunt Sylvia?" Carrie and I asked anxiously. Maybe that was the reason Marilyn was coming home alone. Maybe Marilyn and Darrell had fallen out of love already. "Is the honeymoon over?"

"Well, I guess it is, officially," replied Aunt Sylvia. "But that's not why she's coming home without Darrell."

"Sylvia," Dad said, "why don't you just spit it out."

"Spit what out?" asked Jimmy, still running his finger around the rim of the cake plate.

Aunt Sylvia put her fork down, dabbed her mouth with the paper napkin Mom had handed her, and said,

"Well . . . Marilyn asked me to keep it a secret because she wanted it to be a big surprise, but now she's coming home you'll know anyway."

"Know what?" we all asked at once.

"That I'm going to be a grandmother!" she cried. Then she burst into tears.

"What is it, Sissy? What's wrong?" asked Mom anxiously. And Dad blurted out, "Well, congratulations, Grandma!"

"That's it! That's what's wrong. Grandma! I— I'm not ready to be a grandma!"

"Heck," Jimmy said. "You're way too young to be a grandma anyway, Aunt Sylvia."

"Thank you, Jimmy. You're a darling boy. But . . . "

"Oh, Sissy," Mom said, shaking her head in relief. "I'm ashamed of you. You should be thrilled to pieces."

"Well, I am in a way. But that word — grandma — I hate it!"

"Oh, stop it," Mom snapped. "Pick a name you *do* like then. Nana or Gamma or Nanny or . . . "

"I hate all those silly names," Aunt Sylvia snapped back.

"Women," Dad muttered. "You're never happy unless you've got something to worry about."

"He's right for once," Mom said.

"I know." Aunt Sylvia sniffed and wiped her eyes with a corner of the napkin. "But I don't want to be labelled 'grandma'. It sounds so ancient."

Then I said, "My friend Nancy has an aunt who's a grandmother, and her grandchildren call her Zsa Zsa."

"Oh, now I like that." Aunt Sylvia brightened right up and laughed through her tears. "Why, I've even been told I look like Zsa Zsa Gabor."

"And guess who told you that." Dad pointed to himself. "Why, you'll be the most glamorous grandma in Detroit, Michigan."

"Well . . . " Mom rolled her eyes at Dad. "Let's not get carried away. But if you like it, Sissy, then Zsa Zsa it is. By the way, when is Marilyn expecting?"

"Around the end of August," answered Aunt Sylvia.

"Then we'd better get busy. Tomorrow we'll go down to the wool shop on Jefferson and get some baby yarn and start knitting," Mom said.

"I've never knit a stitch in my life," said Aunt Sylvia.

"There's nothing to it. I'll teach you, Sis."

"What colour are you going to knit?" asked Carrie and I.

"Light green," Aunt Sylvia said, "If the baby inherits my Marilyn's strawberry blonde hair, she'll be gorgeous in green."

"Well, I'm glad that's settled," Dad said. "How does Phil feel about Marilyn travelling all that way by herself?"

"Oh, my goodness, he doesn't even know yet." Aunt Sylvia jumped up and ran for the door. Then she stopped, twirled around, and fluffed up her platinum blonde hair. "Zsa Zsa!" she laughed as she slipped out the door.

Dad shook his head and chuckled.

During all the excitement the baby-twins had been as good as gold. But now Jay banged his empty bottle on his high-chair tray and Joy stretched her arms to be picked up. Looking straight at Carrie with her big blue eyes she squealed, "Caw-ie! Caw-ie!"

Mom dropped a spoon with a splash into the dish-

144

pan. "Did you hear that?" she cried.

"She said my name!" screamed my sister. "She said Carrie!"

"It sounded more like a crow cawing to me," Robbie said.

"Me, too," I said.

"You're both jealous," Carrie said, lifting Joy out of the high chair. "Say it again, Joy. Carrie! Carrie!"

"Caw-ie! Caw-ie!" repeated Joy obligingly.

"Darn," I said. Scooping Jay out of his chair I held him two inches from my face and repeated my name over and over. But all he did was laugh and pull my nose.

It took three more days and every spare minute of my time. But it finally paid off. All of a sudden he yelled in his loud, boy-baby voice, "Connie! Connie!" And he pronounced it perfectly!

Chapter 29

Happy Birthday, Babies!

Marilyn arrived home in time for the twins' first birthday. Mom and Aunt Sylvia had made a nice party for them with a few friends and neighbours, including four babies. There wasn't room for everybody in the dining room so we all gathered around the kitchen table. Dad struck a match and lit the two candles. The babies squealed and clapped their hands and Uncle Phil ran around the table taking pictures from every angle with his flash camera. Then, right in the middle of the festivities, Marilyn jumped to her feet and let out a shriek that would shatter glass.

"It's coming!" she cried, "It's coming!" She was standing with her feet apart in a puddle of water, shaking like a leaf.

Aunt Sylvia ran to the phone to call the doctor. Uncle Phil ran out the door to start his car. Then Dad and Mom took hold of Marilyn on either side and helped her out to the waiting car.

Carrie and I automatically took over the twins.

Robbie and Jimmy herded the remaining guests into the living room. And Dad and Mom came back in and cleaned up the kitchen.

Then Mom brought the cake, half blue and half pink, into the living room and set it on the coffee table. Dad re-lit the candles. Carrie and I knelt down between the twins and helped them blow them out. Then we all sang "Happy Birthday." But the thrill and excitement of the twins' first birthday had been completely spoiled.

"That girl," Mom said tut-tutting and shaking her head, "She'd do anything to be the centre of attention."

* * *

Marilyn's baby was born the next afternoon, July 26. So at least it wasn't on our twins' birthday. Aunt Sylvia phoned from the hospital and told Mom all about it. Mom said, "Yes. Oh, yes, Sylvia, that's lovely. Yes, tell Marilyn we love the name. Yes, I'll tell everybody. We're so happy for you all. Bye."

She hung up. "It's a girl," she said. "And her name is Summertime."

"Balderdash," Dad exploded. "That's not a name, it's a season."

"Well, it's this baby's name so don't you go spoiling it," warned Mom.

"Jay's not a real name either," Jimmy said. "It's a bird."

"And Joy's not a name," Robbie added. "It's a feeling."

"They're all lovely names," Mom insisted.

"And, anyway, Summertime can be shortened to Summer," Carrie and I said.

* * *

One week later we went with Mom to the hospital to see Summertime. The nurse brought her to the nursery

147

window. "Isn't she beautiful?" whispered Aunt Sylvia.

"Just beautiful," Mom agreed.

Carrie and I pulled long faces at each other.

Marilyn's baby had been born a whole month early and only weighed five pounds. Maybe that's why it looked like a wizened-up crabapple with peach fuzz for hair.

Aunt Sylvia leaned over our shoulders. "What do you think of my first grandchild?" she whispered ecstatically.

Carrie and I were tongue-tied. Finally Carrie said, "Well, at least she doesn't look like a skinned rabbit like our babies did."

Then I added quickly, "And they turned out okay."

We knew we'd said the wrong thing when Aunt Sylvia marched away mad and Mom gave us a hard poke in the back.

We didn't hear a word from Aunt Sylvia for a week after that.

Chapter 30

Summer Jobs

With the excitement all over and five whole weeks of summer left before high school, Carrie and I found ourselves at loose ends. Robbie, who was going to college in the fall to study music, was playing in the band at The Blue Moon nearly every night now. He had given up his summer job at the Piggly Wiggly.

"I wish I had a summer job," Jimmy complained, slumping on a kitchen chair. "I need money."

"Well, join the club," Mom said as she sliced carrots on the chopping board. "I'll give you a job. How much do you charge an hour?"

"For what kind of work?" Jimmy asked cagily.

"Well," she scraped the carrots into a pot and started peeling potatoes. "You could cut the grass and weed the garden."

"But Dad always does that," Jimmy said.

"Your dad hasn't got time this summer. He's busy working overtime trying to make the extra money we'll need for moving. So we all have to pitch in and do our bit." She turned the gas on with a pop, adjusted the blue flames, and put the pots on the burners.

"I told you I'm not moving!" insisted Jimmy.

"Then you're going to be awfully lonely here all by yourself." Mom gave the skillet a shake and the meatballs rolled around the pan, spluttering. "You didn't say how much you charge an hour."

"I'm thinking about it," Jimmy said. Then he went into the living room and turned on the Motorola.

"You girls can set the table now," Mom said.

We had no sooner finished than the baby-twins started fighting in the playpen, so we hoisted them up and took them out on the veranda for a swing on the glider.

* * *

After supper there was nothing to do so we went to see if Aunt Sylvia had forgiven us yet. Marilyn was patting Summer on the back, trying to make her burp.

"You have to rub her back," we said.

Marilyn glared at us over Summer's downy red head.

"What are you girls doing for the rest of the summer?" Aunt Sylvia asked in her natural, cheerful voice which told us we were forgiven.

"Nothing much," we answered.

"Well, how would you like a job in my shop? My shampoo girl quit on me and I had to fire my handyman for pilfering so I'm badly in need of help."

"We'd love to, Aunt Sylvia!" we cried.

"But ask your mother first. You know how she hates to be left out of things."

Mom agreed to let us work at The House of Beauty for the rest of the summer. "It'll keep you out of mischief," she said.

150

"You girls should go to hairdressing school," remarked Mrs. Ferguson, Aunt Sylvia's best customer. I was washing her hair and Carrie was taking pink curlers out of the hair of the lady in the next chair. "You're both so good at it."

"Oh, no!" Aunt Sylvia had overheard Mrs. Ferguson. "These girls are going to college, just like their big brother."

"What are you going to study, then?" quizzed Mrs. Ferguson. "Being identical twins, you'll want identical careers, of course."

"No we won't." Carrie dropped the last curler in the tray. "We want different careers because we're individuals."

"I'm thinking of going to teacher's college," I said. The idea had never crossed my mind before.

"I'm going to be a doctor or a scientist," Carrie said. "I haven't decided which yet."

On the way home at the end of the day, Carrie said. "Do you really want to be a teacher?"

"No. I'd rather be a doctor or scientist, too," I said, "but I didn't want Mrs. Ferguson to think she was right."

We worked for the rest of the summer in the beauty shop and we spent all our money on new clothes for high school. We had discovered that if we bought different outfits we could double our wardrobe. So we had decided not to dress exactly alike anymore. Or at least not all of the time.

Chapter 31

Queen for a Day

Real high school turned out to be a lot more exciting than junior high. For instance, the first Friday in October the high school held a "Levi Queen" contest. Carrie and I had bought new Levi's and matching plaid shirts. That was one of our few identical outfits. But we couldn't share the Levi's because Carrie insisted on buying one size smaller than me.

"You'll be sorry," I laughed as she lay flat on her back on the floor trying to squeeze into them.

She finally got them zipped but then she couldn't get up.

"Help me," she cried. "I can't bend."

It took all my strength to pull her to her feet.

Mom took one look at us when we came down to breakfast.

"Turn around," she said to me. I spun around like a top.

"Now you," she told Carrie.

Carrie revolved, as stiff as a wooden soldier.

"Tsk, tsk, tsk," Mom said, pursing her lips. "You'd better not wear those jeans in front of your father, that's all I can say."

Carrie drank her orange juice but she pushed away her porridge.

"You can't go without your breakfast," Mom said.

"I'm not hungry," Carrie insisted. "I'll make up for it at suppertime."

"Promise?"

"Promise."

It took twice as long to walk to school. "Hurry up," I said, "or we'll be late and get detentions."

"I can't bend my knees." She was walking stiff-legged, like a person on stilts.

The contest was going to be held right after lunch. Carrie didn't eat a bite of lunch.

"Are you all right?" I asked. She looked awful peaky to me.

"I'll be okay after," she said in a breathless whisper.

Fifteen girls entered the contest. We marched onto the auditorium stage in single file and lined up in front of the whole student body. Then, Miss Farley, the gym teacher, walked behind us and held her hand over each of our heads and judged the applause.

Carrie won hands down. As Miss Farley placed the gold-painted cardboard crown on her head, I was swamped with envy. How could she have won, I thought, when we looked exactly alike?

The prize was a gold statuette wearing a miniature crown. It looked like a cross between Miss America and the Statue of Liberty. "Thank you, Miss Farley," whispered Carrie. Then she fainted.

* * *

The principal made me sit with her in the nurse's office until she recovered. Then I had to take her home and I missed drama class, which I loved.

Carrie unzipped her jeans underneath her coat and managed to totter home.

"Serves you right," I said, holding onto her hand.

"It was worth it," she whispered, clutching the statuette.

Mom took one look at her white face and sent her straight to bed. Then she confiscated her Levi's and they were never seen again. But I got to keep mine.

Chapter 32

Identical Thoughts

We continued to work Saturdays at The House of Beauty. Mom said it was okay as long as our grades didn't suffer. Aunt Sylvia paid us two dollars each. It made us feel really grown up, earning our own spending money.

All over the beauty-shop walls and taped on the mirrors were pictures of Summertime. She had improved in each new picture and we had to admit she was getting cute. Almost as cute as our twins.

Carrie was removing hot curlers from Mrs. Brewin's crispy white hair. "How old are you girls now, Connie?" Mrs. Brewin asked Carrie.

Carrie didn't bother to correct her. "We'll be fifteen on our next birthday," she answered. Our next birthday was half a year away but Carrie didn't tell Mrs. Brewin that.

"How time flies!" exclaimed Mrs. Brewin. "Why it seems like only yesterday that you were little twin toddlers. And now you are both young ladies. But you still look exactly alike."

We heard this so often that we just smiled and didn't say anything.

* * *

After standing all day we were tired. It was hard work being a hairdresser. So we meandered home slowly up Newport Street, not talking, just thinking our own thoughts. We stopped in front of our house.

Dad had just finished painting the veranda forest green with white railings. Mom had made new cushion covers, in bright fall colours, for the glider. Our parents had been busy as beavers for months now, beautifying our house, getting it ready to sell. It had never looked so beautiful.

Carrie gave a sudden deep sigh, so deep that it made me stare. We looked at each other and the gold flecks in her eyes were like sparks in a fire.

"Are you thinking what I'm thinking?" she almost whispered.

"Maybe," I said. "What are you thinking?"

"Well, I'm thinking that by the time Jay and Joy are as old as we are now, we'll be grown-up women. And Robbie will be over thirty."

That was exactly what I had been thinking. "And even Jimmy will be grown up," I added.

"We'll probably all be married and have homes of our own," Carrie said.

"So why do they need a bigger house?" we asked each other.

A delicious cooking smell wafted down the hall as we came in the door. Mom had made a family favourite, sausage stew. Crisp little sausages bobbed around the frying pan like fat minnows in a pond of golden brown gravy. Carrot rings floated among the sausages like orange waterlilies. And cubes of potatoes and tiny green peas filled the big iron skillet to the brim.

Everybody was home and the table was already set so we all sat down and dug in. The stew disappeared like magic. Dad mopped his plate with a heel of bread until it shone.

"There's no dessert tonight," Mom said apologetically as she poured the tea. "I intended to make baked custard but the twins drank all the milk. They just love the mugs with the spouts that Sylvia gave them," — they were finally off the bottle — "so somebody will have to run out and get some more milk after supper."

"I'll have cheese and crackers," Dad said, contentedly patting his stomach.

"Can I have jam on toast, Mom?" asked Jimmy.

"Help yourself," Mom said as she spooned applesauce out of Gerber jars into the gaping baby-bird mouths of the twins.

Jimmy got the toaster down from the cupboard and we all followed suit and had jam on toast for dessert.

Wiping strawberry jam off her mouth with a paper napkin, Carrie said, "Connie and I have been thinking."

"No, kidding. What about?" quipped Robbie.

We ignored him and spoke together, "Well, we were thinking that when the baby-twins are our age, the rest of us will be all grown up and moved away."

"Moved away!" cried Mom.

"Sure," I said. "So why would you and Dad need a bigger house?"

Everything went silent. You could have heard a fly land, except that it was early fall and the flies were all gone. The only sound that broke the silence was the babies sucking on their spouts.

Mom frowned. "I hadn't even though of that," she said. "But what would we do in the meantime?"

Dad stopped stirring his tea. "Hmmm," he murmured. Then he glanced at Mom. She was gazing around the kitchen. "I've always loved my big farm kitchen," she said in a nostalgic voice. Then she glanced down the hall, "And my French doors, too," she added.

"A man's house is his castle," Dad declared.

Mom rolled her eyes. "But what would we do about that big monstrosity out in no-man's-land?" she said.

All eyes swung towards Dad. His brow was furrowed in a big frown which meant he was thinking deeply. He ran his fingers through his thin, sandy-coloured hair. Finally he spoke, "It's not finalized yet," he said. "And I think I've got an idea."

"What idea?" Mom said.

"Tell us your idea, Dad!" Carrie and I said.

"Well, with the money we've saved up for the down payment on that 'big monstrosity,'" he said, "we could probably fix up the attic. And we wouldn't have to take a second mortgage either."

Connie and I dropped our teaspoons with a clatter and jumped up from the table. "Let's go up and look," we cried.

Dad led the way and we all trooped after him up the stairs.

At the end of the hall on the second floor was a narrow door with a padlock on it. We knew stuff was stored up there, stuff that wasn't used anymore but was too good to throw away.

Dad opened the padlock with a rusty key. He flipped on a switch inside the door and a dusty lightbulb revealed a long narrow staircase trapped between two soaring walls with peeling wallpaper. The stairs creaked as we followed Dad up in single file. He opened the door at the top and flipped another switch. Two bulbs inside the door shone dimly, through cobwebs.

The attic, like the veranda, ran the full breadth of the house. It had small dormer windows at each end, but not much light came in because of the fall leaves flapping against them. Big, sloping beams held up the peaked ceiling.

The room was stuffed to the rafters with junk: old furniture and stacks of boxes and piles of magazines and old clothes hanging on a wire line. Two big steamer trunks stood against the wall and a patchy old rocking horse stared at us with one smoky glass eye.

Mom looked around in dismay. "What would I do with all this stuff?" she worried.

"I could build a storage-shed at the end of the yard," Dad said.

"Those little windows don't let in much light," Mom said.

"I'll trim the trees back," Dad said. Then he gazed up at the peaked ceiling. "A skylight would work wonders up there," he added.

Suddenly a bat swooped down from the highest peak and we all screamed and ran laughing down the stairs.

* * *

After our baths that night, Carrie and I went downstairs in our pyjamas.

The baby-twins were in bed and Robbie was home

because The Blue Moon was closed for renovations. He still played in the band but only on weekends since he'd started college. So he and Jimmy were playing gin rummy for money at the dining-room table. Ever since he'd played poker in Toronto and won money, Jimmy loved playing cards. Mom was afraid he'd turn out to be a card shark when he grew up.

The Motorola had a blank face for a change. Mom and Dad were sitting side by side on the sofa with a big blue paper, the size of a sheet of bristol board, rolled out on the coffee table in front of them.

"What is this?" asked Carrie and I, pointing to the blue paper, which was covered in white lines and numbers.

"Sit down," Dad said, patting the sofa cushion. I sat beside him and Carrie sat beside Mom.

"It's the blueprint of our house," Dad explained. "See . . . here's the downstairs and here's the upstairs and here's the attic." On a notepad he was copying down the measurements of the attic. "I'm trying to figure out what materials I'd need to fix it up," Dad said. "There's enough space up there for two rooms."

Carrie and I leaned forward and looked at each other past our parents. "Whose rooms?" we asked.

Mom answered instead of Dad. "Well, you two have had to share everything all your lives, from the crib to the bunk beds. So we thought it might be a nice change for you to have your own space. Unless, of course, you can't bear to be separated."

"Oh, we can bear it!" we cried ecstatically.

"That settles it then." The blueprint crackled as Dad rolled it up. "I'll get some contractors in to see what they'd charge to do the rough work. Then I'll finish the job myself."

"When would you have time?" Mom asked.

"I've got three weeks holidays coming to me," he said.

"But, Dad, you were saving those holidays to go to Washington next summer," Carrie said.

"Yeah, Dad, you promised someday you'd take us to see the White House," Jimmy reminded him.

Dad had been talking about visiting the President for years.

"Well, the baby-twins will still be too young for such a long trip," Dad said. "And now that Sylvia's a grandmother she won't have time to mind them the way she used to."

It was true. Ever since Summertime had been born Aunt Sylvia almost never came over to give Mom a hand.

"And I wouldn't leave them with anyone else," Mom said. Then she added, "They're getting to be an awful handful for one person. So I'm going to need more help from you girls."

"Oh, we'll help, Mom, we don't mind," we assured her. Ever since the twins had become middle-aged babies, we older twins had grown more and more fond of them.

"What about the bat?" Jimmy asked. He and Robbie had stopped playing cards to listen.

"I'll get rid of it," Dad said.

"You won't have to kill it, will you, Dad?" worried Jimmy. Jimmy was an animal lover who wouldn't kill a fly.

Then Robbie said, "Don't worry, Sport. I'll catch it in a net and set it free."

"Promise?" asked Jimmy.

"Promise," agreed Robbie.

Chapter 33

A Miracle

The transformation of the attic was like a miracle. Light poured in through the two skylights: moonbeams at night and sunshine by day. And Mom had found the time to make new curtains for the dormer windows and bedspreads to match. And Dad had bought us new furniture. Single beds! Mine was silver birch and Carrie's was natural pine.

But the biggest miracle of all was yet to come. The landing at the top of the stairs, which separated our rooms, was itself a small room.

"We could store our big old desk there," I said. "We don't need it now we've got new ones."

"It could be made into a walk-in closet," suggested Mom. "I could certainly do with more closet space."

"I could use it for a music room," Robbie said. Besides his guitar he had acquired a set of drums that took up half the boys' room. Mom said the noise of the drums was enough to waken the dead.

"No way!" Carrie and I protested.

"Well, I got the smallest space in the house," Jimmy piped up, "so if I get my own television for my birthday it could be my television room."

"Dream on, Sport," scoffed Robbie.

While we were all speculating about what to do with the wasted space at the top of the stairs, Dad hadn't said a word. Then he started to chuckle.

"What's funny?" Mom asked him. "You look like the cat that swallowed the sparrow."

"I think you mean canary, Mom," Jimmy said.

Dad just kept on chuckling as if he was hiding something.

"What are you laughing at, Dad?" cried Carrie and I. We were losing patience.

"Well, I was thinking about something . . . " he stroked his chin and paused so long all five of us started shouting at once, "What? What were you thinking about?"

"About a bathroom," he finally said.

"A bathroom! Up there?" Mom sounded incredulous.

"Well, the girls can't be stumbling down that long staircase in the middle of the night," Dad explained. "If they ever tripped they'd break their necks."

Three weeks later, Carrie and I had our own bathroom between our two bedrooms, with a door on either side. The bathroom wasn't big enough for a bathtub so Dad had put in a shower stall with a glazed door you couldn't see through. The toilet and sink were salmon pink and the floor had a grey carpet on it, soft as a towel.

The first night we slept in our own rooms was a strange and thrilling experience.

I could only remember one time when we had been

separated. It was the time Carrie had got hurt in a car accident and had to spend a week in the hospital; the time my identical blood had saved her life. I was awake for hours that first night gazing around my room. My room. I couldn't get over how quiet it was. I couldn't hear a thing: not Carrie's breathing or Dad and Robbie snoring (Robbie looked like Mom but he snored like Dad) or Mom hushing the baby-twins or Jimmy stumbling to the bathroom as he always did in the middle of the night. It was as if I were alone in the world. It was a strange, almost eerie feeling.

I looked up at the sloped ceiling. My skylight was chock full of stars.

"Star light, star bright," I whispered. Then my door opened quietly on its new hinges.

"Connie, are you awake?"

It was my twin sister. My eyes had become accustomed to the night light and I could see the gold flecks sparkling in her green eyes.

"Yes, I'm awake," I said.

"Move over," she said and climbed in bed beside me.

"Are you lonely?" I asked, putting my arms around her.

"Not exactly," she answered, hugging me back.

"Are you scared?"

"Not exactly. Are you?"

"Not exactly."

We didn't need to explain. We understood exactly.

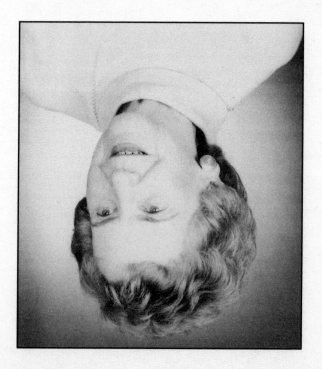

BERNICE THURMAN HUNTER was a storyteller from an early age, but it was not until her children were grown that she began to get her work published. Soon she became one of Canada's favourite writers of historical fiction for children, with a dozen books to her credit, including the best-selling *Booky* and *Margaret* trilogies, *Lamplighter*, *Janey's Choice*, *Two Much Alike*, and *Amy's Promise*, winner of the 1997 Red Cedar Award. In 1989 Bernice received the Vicky Metcalf Award for her contribution to Canadian children's literature, and in 2002 she was appointed to the Order of Canada.